Much Ado *about* Prom Night

Much Ado about Prom Night

WILLIAM D. McCANTS

Browndeer Press
Harcourt Brace & Company
San Diego   New York   London

Requests for permission to make copies
of any part of the work should be mailed to:
Permissions Department, Harcourt Brace & Company,
6277 Sea Harbor Drive, Orlando, Florida 32887-6777.

Browndeer Press is a registered trademark of
Harcourt Brace & Company.

Library of Congress Cataloging-in-Publication Data
McCants, William D., 1961–
Much ado about prom night/written by
William D. McCants.—1st ed.
p.   cm.
"Browndeer press."
Summary: Political uproar about a peer counseling program
in a southern California high school keeps two star-crossed
antagonists at odds before the upcoming prom.
ISBN 0-15-200083-6—ISBN 0-15-200081-X (pbk.)
[1. California—Fiction.   2. High schools—Fiction.
3. Schools—Fiction.   4. Dating (Social customs)—
Fiction.   5. Peer counseling—Fiction.]   I. Title.
PZ7.M47836Mu   1995
[Fic]—dc20   94-43349

The text was set in Simoncini Garamond.
Designed by Trina Stahl
First edition
A B C D E

Printed in Hong Kong

*For my family
and L*

Chapter 1

IT WAS A FRIDAY in mid-April and rays of golden morning sunshine streamed into my cubicle in the peely, creaky white trailer that served as the office for the Peer Counseling Network (PCN) at Luna Point High. My first counselee was Eddie Ballard, a longtime acquaintance and distressingly frequent visitor. He launched our session by asking: "So, Becca, have you got a date to the junior prom yet?"

No big surprise here. With only three weeks to go until the big event, this was fast becoming *the* hot question on campus. I didn't always answer such personal queries from counselees, but I'd served with Eddie on the Luna Point High *Beacon,* our school newspaper, for over two years before I quit at the end of last term, so I smiled and said, "I'll be going with Peter, natch. What's up with you today?"

Eddie flashed me the lopsided grin, which'd lured more than a few girls (mostly unwary ninth and tenth graders) into his octopuslike embrace, as he combed through his thick black hair with his fingers. His gray-blue eyes twinkled. "I just like seeing your face before school starts," he said with a wink.

"That's a really sweet thing to say," I told him. I was shifting into peer counselor mode now, where it's important to always be polite, no matter how heinously you're provoked. Eddie was small for his age and thin as a blade of dune grass. He was the only child of two greenback-cranking, chronically busy parents. My theory was that he was lonely and painfully insecure and tried to compensate for these problems by acting for all the world as if he had *the* hot inside tip on life. The results were predictably disastrous: he came off as a total dork. Whatever the proper diagnosis, his case was clearly way out of my league.

"Didn't you tell me the last time you came in that you've got access to a private therapist?" I asked him. "I think you're really lucky that way, Eddie, and I want to encourage you to take advantage—"

"But my therapist isn't nice like you are," he protested with a sudden—and seemingly genuine—burst of little boy charm and vulnerability. "Besides, he thinks I hate my mother. . . . Do you think I hate my mother, Becca?"

"You're coming off the wall again," I replied impatiently. Eddie liked to try to string out our sessions by messing with my head, but I usually caught him at it.

"Okay, I'll cut to the chase. I had a dream last night that I pushed Jeff Gardiner off Luna Point and he fell a hundred and fifty feet to his death on the foaming rocks below. His skull cracked open like a poached egg. What d'you suppose it means?"

Ouch! How very *Lord of the Flies!* Jeff was the domineering, hard-to-figure, sock-meltingly gorgeous, supertalented editor in chief of the *Beacon,* who seemed to take fiendish delight in writing editorial attacks against the peer counseling program.

"Dream analysis isn't an exact science, not by a long shot," I told Eddie in my professional voice. "Lots of therapists think that dreams reflect a current emotional hang-up; maybe you've been feeling, or repressing, some heavy-duty hostility toward Jeff lately. Or your dream might be construed as a straightforward wish fulfillment, although I'm sure in your conscious state there's no way you'd actually want to send someone sailing over a cliff. . . ."

Eddie seemed undecided on this issue.

"Well," I quickly went on, "*other* experts blow off dreams completely, saying they're just your basic random images awkwardly pieced together by a muddled brain shut off from sensory input. The important thing is, what do *you* think pushing Jeff off a cliff means?"

"An insanity plea, I suppose, unless my lawyers can convince the jury it was an accident," Eddie said solemnly, and then we both laughed.

"Is Jeff still running the paper like a medieval fiefdom?"

"Oh sure, but I don't mind that. He turns out a good product. In fact, I think you'll find this month's issue a real grabber; it should be out by lunchtime."

"It'll be the highlight of my day," I said dryly.

"What bothers me," Eddie went on, getting back to the core of the matter, "is that when I asked Darla Swanson to the prom earlier this week, she turned me down and used Jeff as an excuse." Eddie twisted the band of his Gucci timepiece.

"But why wouldn't she? Jeff *is* Darla's boyfriend!" I steamed, forgetting for a sec about professional detachment. Darla, the features editor of the *Beacon,* had the kind of looks that turn most guys into Play-Doh. She'd had to work on Jeff Gardiner for almost a year, though, before he finally looked up from his computer terminal and clued in to the fact that she was more than just a lively source of ideas for human-interest stories. (Maybe his obliviousness was part of what attracted her to him in the first place.)

"But I can't understand it!" Eddie exclaimed, putting one hand to his chest as he gestured with the other (what a total ham bone!). "Darla's a seven-course dinner at the Ritz-Carlton, a first-run show at the Center for the Performing Arts, a leisurely stroll on Balboa Island at sunset, a vacation condo on Catalina Island! Jeff, on the other hand, is so . . . so—"

"Middle class?"

"Exactly!"

And Eddie was such an outrageous snob, I just had to smile. "It's a burden that many of us shoulder, Sir Edward, but somehow we struggle along. Since you came in for my advice, I've gotta tell you flat out that your flagrant disrespect for a romantic bond, especially such a long-term one (Jeff and Darla'd been a couple for almost six months), bites in the extreme. Besides, I thought Jeff was your bud."

Eddie picked an imaginary piece of lint off his white Ralph Lauren Polo shirt and actually looked a bit sheepish. "I suppose he is. I mean, he always remembers my birthday, even when nobody else does, and he never, ever jokes about my height . . . but it's not as if we hang at lunch together every day. And besides, you haven't seen the way Darla's been sniping at him lately. I hoped she might be looking for an out." There was a sudden clicking sound, and Eddie fished a recorder out of his pocket, popped out the microcassette, and then put a fresh one in.

"Have you been taping this session without letting me know?" I asked, majorly appalled.

"I tape everything. Why, does that bother you?"

I stood up abruptly and said coolly, "Eddie, this meeting is history. If your hostility toward Jeff persists, I recommend you talk it over with a school guidance counselor or your own private therapist. You're really far too complex a case for my modest talents."

He stood up and leaned way over the desk to gaze into my eyes. "Don't sell yourself short, Rebecca darling," he said. "Fact is, except for that little zit on the right side of your nose, you're not a bad-looking girl." He winked at me again. "And once that unfortunate blemish clears up, maybe we could get together socially and—"

What a total slimewad! I removed myself from the cubicle at that point, for safety reasons. *His* safety. (I have this slight tendency to get physical when I'm pushed, and this retreat-and-regroup strategy'd been recommended by my guidance counselor, Mr. Gordon.) Eddie finally got the hint, and once he was good and gone, I excused myself from the waiting students on the threadbare green couch in the reception area and rushed to the nearest bathroom to see about that zit.

~

Adriana Fernandez, my next visitor, tugged at her gold necklace as if it were a noose and told me about the massive crush that she'd developed on her guy friend Omri. "For a long time he was just a bud, you know, until this one afternoon a few weeks ago when we were hanging out in his room listening to a Pearl Jam CD. Omri was doing that stupid air guitar bit that guys are so hooked on, but suddenly the routine seemed kind of clever to me, and later I noticed his fine chin and the cute way he licked the orange Chee-tos dust off his fingers. I felt all tingly and started perspiring, even though it wasn't hot in his room at all."

Adriana nervously gathered her long black hair up into a ponytail and then let it drop down to her shoulders again. "I'm thinking maybe this is all a temporary thing that will pass quickly, you know, like a cold? But then a few days later when I read over the rough draft of his latest English essay, I had the distinct impression it was about me and not Jane Austen."

"You're officially obsessed," I said, smiling.

Adriana made a pained attempt to smile back. "But Omri is totally oblivious! He thinks nothing about us has changed! *I* want to ask him to the prom, but I also don't want our friendship to be ruined if he says no. What can I do?"

We were getting this type of question a lot at the PCN lately, from both girls and guys. (We also talked to quite a few students who were getting unwanted attention from guy friends or girl friends.) "First of all, Adriana, there's nothing strange going on here. Tons of romantic relationships start out as friendships. In fact, my boyfriend Peter and I sang in chorus together for over two and a half years before things finally clicked."

Adriana looked relieved. The people who came to see me almost always seemed to think their problems were unique and therefore something to be ashamed of. It made me feel especially good when I could draw on my own personal experience to help out a counselee, instead of just relying on the secondhand insights I'd snagged from psych class, PCN training sessions, and a humongous stack of adolescent counseling manuals.

"But you've got to play your hand cautiously," I went on, "and even then there are no guarantees. If you don't want to ask Omri straight-out about his feelings for you, then maybe you could try a few pseudodates—you know, long drives together, walks at the beach, some carefully chosen flicks. Keep the conversation light and unthreatening. And whatever you do, don't stalk him at school!"

Adriana nodded firmly.

"If you feel like taking a bigger risk, get a friend of yours to tell a bud of his about your feelings and see what comes back to you. If Omri turns chilly, slack off, and the damage to your friendship should be minimal."

"But isn't there a quicker way to find out if he feels the same way I do?" she asked desperately.

I had to think for a moment. No ready answer to that one. "Maybe. Body language can sometimes speak volumes. The next time you're deep in conversation with Omri, touch him on the arm, the shoulder, or if you're feeling super brave, the face. If he flinches and draws back, the feeling is almost definitely not mutual, but if he smiles at you, or better yet, reciprocates—"

"I've got him!" she said excitedly as she smacked her fist into her open palm. Adriana was hunched forward now, her eyes alive with schemes and strategies. Then she bit her thumbnail. "But what about the prom?"

"You mean what if the feedback you've gotten from Omri is still nebulous and the big dance looms . . . ? I'd ask him to go as a friend. Stress that the prom is no big deal, but you think it could be fun anyway. That'll take the pressure off both of you, and then when you're all decked out in traffic-stopping formal wear and carving up that ballroom dance floor together, who knows?"

Adriana was smiling now. "You got a date?"

I smiled back.

As she got up to leave, though, she began frowning again and said, "What if I do all this stuff you suggest, and then when he eventually finds out how I really feel about him, he still freaks on me?"

"You can sue me for every penny I've got," I said, and she laughed.

"Seriously, Adriana," I went on, "this isn't

an exact science I'm practicing here. I'm just around to hear you out and try to give you a few informed tips on how to tackle your vexing probs." I pointed to a poster hanging on the back wall of the cubicle, a killer work of art I'd coaxed out of Lance Hughes, the *Beacon* cartoonist (the concept and the cautionary slogan were my two contributions). On it was a tennis player who'd tossed his racket into the air and was about to take a swing at it with his ball. "WE AIM TO SERVE," the caption read, "BUT WE DON'T ALWAYS GET IT RIGHT."

⌒

Chip Windeman was wearing a rainbow-colored knitted cap, a red-plaid flannel shirt, faded blue jeans with holes in the knees, and a deep scowl. "That Zoner guy, his schedule is full up," Chip grumbled.

"I know and I'm sorry." Zoner was one of our most popular counselors. "But maybe I can help you," I said.

Chip whipped out a Swiss army knife, extracted the scissors, and began clipping his fingernails. "You're a girl," he said accusingly as he worked on his thumbnail.

"That's a good start," I said, nodding with encouragement. "So far we're in complete agreement."

The clipping stopped for a moment, and Chip gave me a hard look. I held his gaze until he finally turned away. He closed up the knife, slapped it down on the desktop, and said, "Do you *personally* talk to many guys here?"

I nodded. "Not as many as Zoner and the other boy counselors, but I get my share."

Chip pulled off the cap and began to work it between his hands. His dark brown hair was matted to his scalp; grunge all the way. "This girl Flora wants me to ask her to the prom, and I really like her a lot, but I just don't have the bucks." He looked up at me sharply, as if daring me to make fun of him. When I didn't, his features softened, along with his voice. "Flora's got smoky eyes, and she smells like wild raspberries," he explained. "She writes song lyrics and wants to be an oceanographer." He gazed at me warily again.

"She sounds real special."

He grinned and nodded. "I bag groceries at this market down by the marina. The pay's fair, but most of it goes to rent and my car. I live with my grandma, see, and she's on Social

Security. Anyway, I've been checking out what the prom costs, and it's mind-blowing! Tickets, tux, dinner, limo, corsage—we're talking three hundred dollars and up! I wanna do right by Flora. Like you said, she's real special. But three hundred dollars is way beyond my reach. And you wanna know what? I've heard about some couples around here who're planning to shell out a thousand bucks or more! How's that possible?"

I shook my head. If I got into social class comparisons, I'd be worthless as a peer counselor at Luna High. "Let's focus on your problem, Chip. Can you see any solutions?"

"Well, no. . . . That's why I'm here!" he said irritably.

I held my hand up in a calming gesture. "My point is, the way you've got this figured, there *is* no solution. So you've gotta *rethink* the problem. D'you know, for instance, that a lot of girls are more than happy to pay their own way these days, and some even fork out for the guy, too? It depends in part on who's got the loot."

Chip had to ponder that a bit. It was obviously a new concept for him. "Flora's not rich, if that's what you mean—," he began.

"Neither of you has to be wealthy to make the prom happen. You just have to be realistic and resourceful. Is a limo out of your price range? Okay, then why not just wax up your own car and take Flora in that—"

"My wheels are in prime condition already," Chip said defensively. I looked at the desktop and noticed that his nail clippings were black. Grease.

"Then you're halfway there," I said with a smile. "And you can skip the fancy restaurant, too, if you want. Go for quality over price. It may take some extra time, but if you search long and hard enough, you're bound to find bargain rental rates on a tux. Or you could get creative, go to a secondhand clothing store and let your imagination run wild."

Chip looked down at his clothes and grinned. "Now you're talking," he said. Soon he was spouting out ideas of his own, and by the time the bell rang for first period, he'd decided to ask Flora to the prom right away.

"She's a lucky girl," I told him.

I went off to chem class, confident that Peter would make me feel just as lucky.

Chapter 2

KAYLA, ZONER, and I were eating lunch at our favorite table, the one on the grassy knoll that overlooks Luna High in all its prefab California mission-style glory. It'd turned into a "palm-tree day"—sunny, breezy, and dee-lish. Peter said he'd join us after his debate club meeting, but it must've been running super late.

"How can you be obsessing about the prom, Kayla," Zoner said after wolfing down his second peanut butter and banana sandwich, "when we've got tons of waste floating in orbit, just waiting to bail?"

Kayla turned to me, smiled, and said, "Can

you believe how blatantly this guy changes the subject?"

Zoner had a real talent for coming up with bizarre questions. Last week it was: "If you were going to die exactly one year from now, would you still apply to college in the fall?" And the week before that: "If the black box flight recorder survives even the gnarliest plane crashes, then how come the whole airplane isn't built like the black box?"

"Can you be more specific about this rubbish-in-reentry deal, Professor Zoner?" I asked him.

"Why, of course," he said as he pulled some of his long, straggly bleached-out hair away from his deeply tanned face and straightened out his faded burgundy LIFE'S A BEACH tank top. "The U.S. Space Command is currently tracking over seven thousand pieces of space junk that are the size of a baseball or larger. Seven percent of these objects are satellites and fifteen percent of them are spent rocket bodies—"

"Spent rocket bodies?" Kayla asked with a giggle.

"That's right, young lady," Zoner affirmed with NASA spokesmanlike formality. "And while I'd hate to fill that pretty strawberry blond head of yours full of worry, we can't dismiss the statistical possibility that there's a satellite up there with your name on it."

We all laughed together, and I noticed that Kayla's lagoon-blue eyes lingered on Zoner a little longer than usual. The three of us'd been friends since Zoner had helped Kayla and me learn to surf at a beach day camp the summer after junior high. (He'd also introduced us to surfspeak, a sort of second language that Kayla and I could now lapse into whenever the spirit moved.) His real name was Terry Kingman; the nickname came from his general off-the-wallness, as well as his uncanny knack for finding a surfable zone in waves that others thought unridable.

"I still don't see why you're so down on the prom, Zoner," Kayla said, going doggedly back to the previous discussion.

"I have nothing against the prom," he said good-naturedly. "I just think that if God meant guys to dress up like penguins, He'd've given us webbed feet and a craving for squid."

When I laughed and Kayla didn't, Zoner turned to me and said, "Help me out here,

Becca. You don't think the prom is the be-all
and end-all, do you?"

"You're asking the wrong person," I told
him. "I *want* the fairy-tale thing, the whole
Cinderella transformation. I've had my dress
picked out for ages; it's a Sylvia Casimiro design in pink lace, and I've been saving up for
it for almost six months. I want the limo, the
flowers, the dinner; I want to feel like a prin-
cess. You can dis the prom all you want, big
guy, but some of us still believe in magic, and
we're not gonna apologize for it."

"Outstanding defense, Becca!" Kayla said
gleefully as we exchanged a high five.

"This session is a bust," Zoner conceded,
throwing up his hands.

As a goodwill gesture, I offered Zoner the
avocado and garbanzo bean pita-pocket sandwich my mom had foisted off on me that
morning, but he turned it down. ("This could
be the hot ticket to finally improving your skin
tone," Mom'd said cheerfully, as if I'd *known*
there was a problem with my skin tone.)

"Yo, Becca!" Peter called out as he trudged
up the knoll. My boyfriend was tall, a little
husky, and had short, shiny gold-streaked

brown hair with bangs that never behaved. He looked like a big teddy bear. As a debater, he specialized in health-care issues, and he was a terrific booster for the PCN, even though he didn't have either the time or the inclination to be a counselor himself. He'd captured my heart not because of his tenor singing voice, which was only so-so, but because of his zesty, go-for-it personality. Two months ago he'd invited me to the Valentine's dance by handing me a bouquet of red roses, and I'd been hooked on him ever since.

Of course, Peter wasn't without his flaws; none of us are. What bugged me most was his tendency to flirt flagrantly with pretty girls. Lately he'd been spending an inordinate amount of time with a perky ninth-grade debater named Cindy Silber. Peter insisted that Cindy was just eager to "learn the ropes" from him, and that sounded plausible enough to me, even though it was getting to the point where she probably saw more of him on a daily basis than I did. I tried not to make too much of an issue out of it, though, because I figured if you can't trust your own boyfriend, you've got major problems.

"Sorry I'm so late," Peter said as we

hugged each other. He pulled away more quickly than usual. *Body language?* "We got caught up in discussing the legal issues surrounding terminal illness and then the *Beacon* was delivered," he explained as he caught his breath. (Peter wasn't into physical exertion, unless you counted making out, and so, much to Zoner's and Kayla's outspoken annoyance, I'd had to let my surfing slide over the past few months.) "You're not gonna like it, Becca."

I seized the copy of the paper that Peter offered me, and while he gabbed with Zoner and Kayla, I turned directly to the editorial page, to Jeff's column. This month it was entitled:

THE PEER DELUSION NETWORK: WHO NEEDS IT?

In December the so-called Peer Counseling Network opened its doors to the students of Luna Point High School. In a column written at that time, I questioned the need for such a service, as well as the qualifications of the student volunteers staffing it. But after a modest start, the PCN, started by former *Beacon* staffer Rebecca Singleton, soared in popularity.

In February I reexamined the network in

terms of issues of trust and confidentiality, wondering if your secrets would really be safe in the hands of a group of teen non-professionals who were subject on a daily basis to the same fierce social pressures that dog us all. I was intrigued to see some decline in patronage after that column appeared, but the PCN gradually recovered and now seems more vital than ever.

And, of course, why wouldn't it be, in this age of talk-show journalism and injustice collecting? Aren't we Americans taught now that we are all victims? If we face a crisis in our lives, especially one of our own making, aren't we encouraged to see a lawyer or a shrink (or a peer counselor) so that they can quickly assign the blame elsewhere?

Can the time really be far off when a student, unsuccessful in his or her quest for a prom date, will be able to sue a high school for "pain and suffering"? . . .

I read this attack piece to its bitter end and then threw the paper down in disgust. "Once again, that reptile Jeff Gardiner is totally misrepresenting what we're trying to do! And just like last time, he gave me no advance notice, so I had no chance to write a counterpoint column! I can't believe he had the gall to run this right in the middle of prom season, when so many people are feeling vulnerable!"

Peter, Kayla, and Zoner tried to calm me down and reassure me that almost nobody took Jeff's column very seriously, but I knew better and so did they (especially Zoner, who used to write the occasional surf story for the *Beacon*). Jeff's first attack had nearly smothered the network in its infancy, and after the second one we'd been mobbed by panicked counselees who were worried that their secret life crises were being illegally traded on the Luna High gossip exchange.

He knew full well I'd gotten the idea to start the PCN last spring when three guidance counseling positions fell under the budget ax. Those cuts happened in spite of a four-part series I'd just written on teen problems at Luna High— problems like suicidal depression, coping with divorce, and facing unplanned pregnancies. I'd thought about how much family therapy helped me after my parents' recent divorce, so with the full-on support of Mr. Gordon (and major assists from Kayla and Zoner), I'd worked through the summer and fall to scrounge together a peer therapy program.

Actually, as far as I was concerned, if even a single troubled teen was kept away from the PCN by Jeff's misleading editorials, that was one too many. It was clearly high time to meet the weenie on his home turf and kick some butt!

⟲

I anxiously watched the clock all through my AP U.S. history class, and then rushed out of the room when the bell rang and ran over to the language building to get excused from British lit. We were studying Shakespeare's play *Much Ado about Nothing*. I'd seen the movie, and Kayla promised she'd share her notes with me later.

I waited outside the open door of the journalism classroom for about five minutes while Jeff got the monthly critique session under way. You might wonder how a junior got to be editor in chief of a high school newspaper. In the spring of last year, when Jeff was still just the opinion page editor, he published a pro-con piece on the merits of making condoms available to the students of Luna High. Then, in the following month, he wrote, with my assistance, a blistering editorial denouncing the planned layoffs of not just guidance counselors but a sizable number of teachers and support staff as well. Bernard Crampton, a school board member, blasted the *Beacon* editorials and called the paper a "one-sided mouthpiece for a liberal political agenda." Citing the board censorship powers granted to school officials over students in the U.S. Supreme Court's 1988 *Hazelwood School District v. Kuhlmeier* decision, Mr. Crampton insisted on the right to review future issues of the *Beacon* for "inappropriate" editorial content.

Jeff was fabulous; he went totally ballistic. He appeared before the board and pointed out that since the *Beacon* had long operated as a pro-con "open forum" for student opinion, the reasoning in *Hazelwood* didn't apply here. He also reminded Mr. Crampton that California law granted students free press rights that were more generous than the post-*Hazelwood* federal standards.

Several staffers, including myself, also helped Jeff to organize a rally against censorship. It featured a speaker from the American Civil Liberties Union and was covered by members of the local media, who of course ate this freedom of expression story right up.

We figured Mr. Crampton either hadn't done his legal homework or he was counting on our ignorance. Big mistake! He finally backed down (but only after a condom distribution proposal for the high school was dropped from the board agenda) and had to settle for speaking his piece in a special all-editorial edition of the *Beacon*.

So scarcely a year ago, when it served a cause *he* was into, Jeff'd manipulated the "talk-show journalists" and "injustice collectors" with the best of 'em.

What a hypocrite!

I walked into the classroom as he was in the midst of holding forth about "journalistic objectivity." The *Beacon*'s faculty advisor, Ms. Sullivan, was sitting at a desk behind Jeff. She favored me with a slight nod and a smile.

I positioned myself at the far end of the enormous meeting table (which was really just a bunch of smaller tables pushed together), directly across from where Jeff was seated, and said, "I'm sorry to interrupt a sermon, Your Worship, but I've come to lodge a complaint."

Jeff froze midsentence and regarded me with startled blue eyes. The twenty or so staff members present turned away from him to look at me, and I was flooded with enthusiastic greetings. (Darla Swanson, though, gave me only a halfhearted wave.)

Jeff recovered quickly. "You see, Becca," he said, "everybody here misses you. You were an awesome journalist. You never should've left."

"Having you as a peer, Jeff, was at times barely tolerable; suffering you as a boss was simply more than I could take," I responded. I picked up a copy of the *Beacon* from the table and tossed it in his direction. "Why another hatchet job on the Peer Counseling Network? Are you really that starved for story ideas? Can't you just go chasing after UFOs like all the other tabloid journalists?"

"I love you, too," Jeff replied, smiling as he clasped his hands behind his head and thrust his chest out. How pathetically transparent! I knew from my exhaustive summer psych reading that this was a classic gesture used by human males in an attempt to assert their dominance; it was right down there on the evolutionary scale with chest-pounding by gorillas. "Face it, Becca," he went on, "our last two shoot-outs in the *Beacon* generated a ton of reader interest, and that's what juicy journalism is all about. I can hardly wait for your next devastating rebuttal."

"Is that supposed to be a compliment?"

"Why—are you in need of one?" he said, as he dropped his pose and stood up to face me. "Has it been too long between award ceremonies? Has the Ivy League stopped calling with scholarship offers?"

"God, I miss this!" Lance Hughes said, and several staffers murmured in agreement.

"The people who come to my trailer don't give a damn about your 'reader interest,' Jeff. They come because they're confused or lonely or somebody hurt them or they hurt somebody and didn't mean to. They come because they know that for fifteen minutes they'll have the undivided attention of another human being. Not everyone has a captive audience like you do."

People laughed again, and Randy Strother, the staff photographer, snapped my picture.

"Wait 'til she throws the first punch, Randy," Eddie Ballard joked.

" 'My trailer,' " Jeff repeated, ignoring the others. "That's kind of revealing, isn't it?"

My face felt very hot suddenly. "Not nearly

so revealing as your vanity editorials!" I replied angrily. Heads at the table were turning to and fro, as if this were a match at
Wimbledon. "You keep blindsiding me, Jeff,
and that's a wussy ploy. You make sure you
have the stage all to yourself for a month at a
time 'cause you're scared your flimsy argument won't stand up to an informed challenge. You don't believe in free speech these
days any more than your old buddy Bernard
Crampton does!"

"Ooooh!" said the staff.

"If you think I'm just posing here, Becca,
you're dead wrong!" he said heatedly. "I honestly believe that therapy's used just to assign
blame arbitrarily and to turn people against
each other."

"Yes, I know; I read your piece, and it was
a great hook! But I need to see your *research,*
Mr. Editor in Chief. 'Opinions are easy; facts
are hard.' Isn't that what you used to say? And
how dare you take a cheap shot at people who
don't have prom dates. That totally sucks!
How insensitive can you be?"

Jeff glanced briefly at Darla, and she looked
away. "Damn it, Becca," he said, pounding his
fist on the table, "all I'm saying is that people

need to take responsibility for their own actions and learn how to handle their own problems! What's so wrong with that idea?"

"Nothing," I said. "Except that most of us weren't born thinking we know all the answers."

Some staff members actually broke into applause this time, but before Jeff could return the volley, the classroom door opened. Mr. Grambeau, the assistant principal in charge of discipline, was looking for me. "It's Roger again," he whispered. "He's in the main office."

"Is this about your little brother?" Jeff asked gleefully as a smile returned to his face. "What's the tiny terror done this time? Set the science building on fire? Started another food fight in the ninth grade caf?"

"Your smugness'll come back to haunt you, Jeff Gardiner," I said.

"HEAD PEER COUNSELOR PLAGUED BY DELINQUENT SIBLING," Jeff announced, using his hands to frame the imaginary headline. "Now *there's* a tabloid story if I ever heard one."

I left quickly with Mr. Grambeau, totally steamed that in spite of my go-for-the-jugular attack on his journalistic ethics, Jeff'd still managed to get in the last jab.

～

"Where'd you get the idea to cut Mr. Limbrick's hair in the first place?" I asked Roger as I drove him home in my ancient, sputtering bronze Olds Cutlass.

Roger ignored me and looked out the window to focus on the street action of Pacific Coast Highway. He'd just recently turned fifteen and smelled of Reese's Pieces and dirty athletic socks. He was wearing, as always, his black leather Hard Rock Cafe jacket, a Christmas gift from our father, who'd moved to New York about a year-and-a-half ago. (Roger'd played a hot keyboard for the school jazz ensemble back in junior high but'd since given it up.) My brother's hair, which up until the end of eighth grade had been a quasi-medium brown with the occasional gold streak like mine, was now shaved on the sides and dyed jet black on top.

"I know Mr. Limbrick is not the best algebra teacher on the planet," I went on. "And even the principal admitted that it was out of line for a faculty member to fall asleep in class.

But that doesn't give you the right to pick up a pair of scissors and—"

"Can I turn on the radio, sis?" Roger turned to me to ask in his usual bored monotone. He had hazel eyes, also like mine, although he was no doubt in the market for a pair of jet black contact lenses.

"No, you can't. Roger, do you realize that you've been *suspended?* When Mom comes home tomorrow from her conference in Sacramento and hears about this, she's going to freak!" (Mom kept a roof over our heads as a public relations exec, but her true love was sculpting, and I think the fact that she had so little time to pursue her art these days worked her nerves in a major way. Roger's constant delinquency only made things worse.)

Roger shrugged at my mention of Mom, but his eyes betrayed some anxiety. "She'll deal with it. She always does. And if not, I'll just go live with Dad."

I gripped the steering wheel a little more tightly and tried to ignore the sudden flutter in my stomach. "Did Dad say you could?"

Roger nodded uncertainly.

I felt helpless. The family therapist that Roger, Mom, and I had gone to after the divorce warned that the transition to high school could be super rough for an adolescent boy with an absent father. "Just be patient with Roger and love him," she advised us. "Allow him his space and as much quality time with his dad as possible."

But Dad, also a public relations exec, was on the road more than ever these days, and Roger had this unfortunate tendency to corrupt or destroy whatever "space" we gave him.

"Can I switch on the radio now. Pretty puhlease?" Roger asked again as he moved the tuning dial to a different station and turned the volume way up.

"No way!" On impulse, I got off the highway and pulled into the parking lot of a 7-Eleven. I parked under a palm tree, shut off the engine, and said, "I know we agreed I'm never supposed to do the peer counseling thing with you. But can't we just *talk* for once, like a brother and sister are supposed to?"

This idea seemed to amuse him. "You mean like the happy, well-adjusted sibs on cable TV reruns? Brenda and Brandon, Alex and Mallory, Marcia and Greg?"

"Exactly," I said.

"Okay," he said gamely as he began scratching various body parts (ahhh, the ravages of testosterone). "I'll go first: Gee, Becca, how come you didn't tell me you broke up with Peter?"

"What?!"

"My friend Tony Zimmerman saw him kissing a girl in the balcony of the auditorium at lunch today, so I figured you two must be couple-toast," Roger said mildly.

"You— I'm sure you— It must've been somebody else," I sputtered.

"No, it wasn't," Roger said confidently. "Tony told me his eyes had adjusted to the darkness, 'cause he was on the other side of the balcony making out with Marcie Scott. It was Peter all right, and he was locking lips with this totally luscious babe from my class— Cindy Silver, I think her name is."

"Silber," I said dully.

Roger studied my face. "This is all news to you, isn't it?" he said, amazed. Then he clapped his hands together and started to laugh uproariously. "That's classic!"

Great. After over a year of trying, I'd finally managed to put Roger in a good mood.

Chapter 3

As a peer counselor I'd seen more than a few relationships trashed by false second- and thirdhand rumors. So as I dropped Roger off at home and motored back to the high school at ambulance speed, I resolved to stay calm, to report the rumor to Peter in a good-humored, matter-of-fact kind of way, and then let him assure me of his innocence so I wouldn't have to kill him.

I found him in the almost-empty debate classroom (school'd let out a while ago). He and Cindy were sitting shoulder-to-shoulder, yukking it up over some item in a magazine they were reading together. I scraped a nearby desk across the floor to announce my presence.

"Hi, Becca!" Peter said when he looked up. "I heard you had to take Roger home. Is everything okay?"

"I sure hope so. Look, Peter, I need to talk to you about something for a minute. Preferably in private."

Cindy looked up and acknowledged me with a brief, tight little smile before going straight back to the mag.

"Sure thing," Peter said cheerfully as he stood up. "Where'd you like to go?"

"How about the balcony in the auditorium?"

Peter blanched and Cindy took on the aspect of a maraschino cherry.

I felt a sudden urge to cry but quickly smothered it. I grabbed my stunned and uncharacteristically silent debate chump by the arm and led him out into the hallway in search of a vacant room. Ms. Attanucci's bio lab was the first available.

"Oh, Peter," I wailed after shutting the door, "how *could* you?!"

"It was Cindy's idea," he blurted out as he backed up against a poster of a dissected frog.

"She came on to me, and I guess I just got caught up in the moment."

I shook my head. "Cliché central. Try again."

It took him forever to come up with something else. "You know," he said as he stepped away from the wall, "it occurs to me that we never actually agreed, at least in a formal way, that we were in an exclusive relationship here. The terms of allowable conduct, therefore, were rather ambiguous. Ergo—"

"Are you *kidding?*" I asked in disbelief, poking his chest with my finger and causing him to back away from me, toward the rear of the classroom this time. "Do you think this is a formal debate or something? (*poke*) I was really falling hard for you, you insensitive clod! (*poke*) I thought you were a guy I could *trust!*" (*poke, poke*) Peter suddenly stumbled and fell to the floor.

"God, I'm really sorry," I said sincerely as I got down on the floor to make sure he was okay.

"Jeez, Becca, why do you have to get so physical when you're mad?"

"I told you before. The family therapist said it was probably displaced aggression left over from my parents' divorce. Mr. Gordon is giving me tips on how to deal. . . . And look who's lecturing *me* about getting physical!" I said, getting mad all over again.

We sat on the dirty tiled floor in silence for a few more minutes.

"If you took our relationship so lightly, Peter, then why'd you have to go and tell me you loved me?" I asked.

He looked puzzled. "When did I say that?"

"In the parking lot at Jack in the Box, just two Saturdays ago! You remember—we went there for dessert after seeing that great Tom Hanks movie. I had an order of cinnamon churritos and you had two slices of chocolate chip cookie-dough cheesecake."

When this still didn't register, I said flatly, "The temp was in the low sixties. There were two other cars in the lot. I think one was a Honda Prelude, and the other was a—"

"Okay! Okay. I remember," he said. "But when a guy says 'I love you,' Becca, especially so early in a relationship, it doesn't necessarily mean what a girl thinks it does."

I was wasting my time. I stood up and slapped the dust off my pants. "Don't generalize about guys with me, Peter. A lot of them know exactly what 'I love you' means, and they're true to it. I suppose I should be grateful, though, that I found all this out *before* prom night."

Peter suddenly looked totally distressed. "You mean you're breaking up with me?" he asked in disbelief. "But I was planning to ask you to the prom this weekend, Becca. I swear I was! Don't you think you're overreacting just a little here? Cindy's only fifteen. A kid, practically. If you really want me to keep things platonic with her from now on, then that's exactly what I'll do."

I thought about Cindy for a moment and the flagrant disregard she'd shown for my romantic bond with Peter. "Don't bother," I said. "I'm sure she deserves what you have to offer way more than I do."

~

On the long drive home, as I kept mopping my tear-soaked face with Kleenex, I tried to remember strategies for handling breakups. It was a no-go. I finally switched on the radio for comfort and got blasted instead:

"Broken families and remote-controlled lives!
Buzzing nowhere in no-exit beehives!
No way to make it in this world on your own!
So give me cable and just leave me alone!"

I'd completely forgotten about Roger changing the station. No wonder the kid was so twisted.

Not wanting to go back to one of my favorite stations, which all put a major stress on upbeat love songs, I raced across the FM band until I crashed into a country-and-western tune:

"My dog was run over by a truck headed
    west;
My farm done gone under, the bank
    repossessed;
But that ain't enough to give me the blues,
Long as I've got my woman and a good pair
    of shoes."

I laughed out loud and cheered up just a bit. No farm, no dog, no guy, but I did have several pairs of great shoes. Maybe I could walk my way through this.

When I felt the reassuring embrace of home, I began to remember some of those elusive steps for coping with heartbreak that I'd studied up on as a peer counselor-in-training.

Step One: Talk to people who care. Roger was KO'd from this category the second he took his microwaved TV dinner lasagna into his room and slammed the door. I called Kayla, but she was apparently out with her family. I called Zoner, but he must've been out with his board. So I left a simple message on each of their answering machines: "Peter cheated on me; please send chocolate."

Step Two: Do something constructive to take your mind off your troubles. After dinner, once the dishwasher was running, I set about cleaning my bedroom. I started by taking down the small photo collage of Peter pictures that hung on the wall just opposite my pillow. I toyed with the idea of shredding every last one of them but found I didn't have the heart for it quite yet. (Couldn't he still surprise me? Show up at my door on his knees, with a bouquet of flowers in his hand, and . . . and more lame rationalizations for his slimy misdeed!) I dusted the furniture and fluffed my quilted bedspread.

As I began to straighten out my awards shelf, I remembered the "award ceremonies" crack that Jeff Gardiner'd made earlier in the day. Which brought me to . . .

Step Three: Do something that makes you feel good. I pulled out last year's high school annual and found Jeff's large photo on page 147. (Jeff'd won an *Orange County Times* citation for excellence in high school journalism, editorial division.) "To Becca," he'd scribbled under the picture in a bold, black hand, "a fearsome foe, a first-class collaborator, and a cherished friend. Love, Jeff." I'd gotten the chills when I first read that, last June. It was evidence for my private theory, long since tossed, that the "real" Jeff Gardiner was a warm, sensitive, caring human being who just needed the love of the right girl to draw him out.

Darla Swanson, though, was not the girl I'd had in mind.

I cut out Jeff's picture, removed the small garbage bag that lined my red-white-and-blue "Great Seal of the President of the United States" trash can (a gift from a relative who had high hopes for my future—and a twisted sense of humor), and then using some transparent tape, carefully affixed Jeff's image to the shiny metal bottom inside the receptacle. I got an amazing amount of pleasure from this petty little act, and it didn't even occur to me to wonder why I was using Jeff's picture instead of Peter's.

"That's really twisted," Roger said over my shoulder.

I hadn't heard him come in my bedroom, and I was so shocked that I literally jumped up from the chair and dropped the can. "Don't you believe in knocking?" I asked, my heart pounding.

"Your door was open," he said calmly. As I picked the can back up, he examined the mutilated yearbook and actually grinned a little. "Finally getting some of those repressed feelings for Jeff Gardiner out of your system, huh? You know, sis, there may be hope for you yet."

I sometimes forgot that Roger and I had gone through four months of family therapy *together*.

"You won't tell anyone?" I said, suddenly feeling very foolish and vulnerable.

"As if," he said, rolling his eyes.

"Thanks," I said, super relieved. "So what's up? You want to talk?"

He shook his head. "I want to invite Chris Bowen over."

"Chris Bowen?" A sophomore. Shaved head. Eats peanuts without removing the shells. "Isn't he in jail?"

"Not anymore. And besides, how was he supposed to know it was against the law to throw live explosives off a public pier?"

I laughed. "Yeah, that's an innocent mistake practically anyone could've made. But he can't come over tonight, armed or unarmed," I said firmly. "You've been suspended."

"You're just ticked at me for passing along the bad news about Peter," Roger said, and then he sulked out of my room.

Was he right? Was I acting out of sisterly concern, or was this just displaced aggression on my part? How could I be sure? I needed a second opinion. An objective judge. A parent, even! But I didn't dare call Mom in Sacramento; she'd take a red-eye flight home and be cranky for weeks. And Dad lived totally out of the loop, a whole continent away.

I put these thoughts aside and went back

to cleaning, which worked like a charm once again until I accidentally came across a snapshot of Peter and me at the Valentine's dance. We looked so happy together. And he seemed so gentlemanly! So trustworthy! I thought about our splendiferous March trip to Catalina Island, when we'd kissed at dusk at Casino Point; the late night yakfests in the Jacuzzi at Carolyn Preimsberger's house; the pork-out sessions at Baskin-Robbins after school on Friday afternoons.

I was in the midst of a second crying jag when the doorbell rang. It was Kayla and Zoner bearing chocolate, plus other decadent goodies. And God bless 'em, they aimed to kidnap me. "I'd come willingly, but I can't leave Roger here alone," I said, explaining about the suspension.

"No worries. I'll just hip the dude to the direness of the situation," Zoner said confidently as he shuffled off in the direction of Roger's room.

Zoner reemerged five minutes later with a smile on his face, as if he'd just snaked his way through a monster barrel, and he gave me a thumbs-up. "There was some resistance at first, but the grom finally decided to flow with it. He'll stay put," Zoner said. "When's he gonna take up surfing, anyway? It could cure what ails him."

"Probably when I give it up," I said grimly.

～

"Primo conditions for a Twinkie roast," Zoner said as we sat around a fire pit at the beach. Before we met Zoner, it'd never occurred to either Kayla or me that a Twinkie *could* be roasted. But they were surprisingly tasty in their blackened state—chewy on the outside, soft and hot and bubbly on the inside. For an extra kick we sometimes dipped them in an open can of Hershey's chocolate syrup.

Going to the beach that night gave my soul a major revamp. The night air was rich with the smell of the black sage and lemonade berry blanketing the nearby hillsides, and you could hear the waves playing their soothing riff as they crumbled into oblivion on the nearby shoreline. Happy surfing memories came to mind as mainland hassles receded. On the eastern horizon, a grinning three-quarter moon peered over the bold, black profile of the Santa Ana Mountains, and I could almost hear the lunar dude telling me, "Cheer up, babe."

"Make sure you pull down and stash everything that reminds you of Peter," Kayla told me.

"Already done," I said.

"Focus on new projects and goals and exercise daily to free up those mood-boosting endorphins," Zoner added.

"I worked up a sweat cleaning my room."

"Be nice to his new girlfriend when you cross paths at school. It'll show how classy you are and confuse the hell out of both of them," Kayla said.

"Spend more time with your buds and remember that you don't need a dude to be a whole and complete person," Zoner said.

"Smile big-time even when you're down. It'll trigger the brain chemicals that bring on happy feelings," Kayla said.

"Go back to surfing at least once a week instead of practically never," Zoner concluded. "Ancient Surf Sage says: ' 'Tis better to charge a peak than date a geek.' "

"Ancient Surf Sage? Puhlease," Kayla said with a laugh.

I laughed, too, and then applauded them

both. "One thing's for certain," I said. "If you're going to get dumped on by life, make sure your best friends are peer counselors."

"Wait! There's one more piece of advice you need to hear," Kayla said, reaching into her backpack and pulling out a paperbound copy of *Much Ado about Nothing*. She turned to the page she wanted, moved closer to the firelight, sat up straight, and read:

> *"Sigh no more, ladies, sigh no more,*
> *   Men were deceivers ever,*
> *One foot in sea, and one on shore,*
> *   To one thing constant never.*
> *Then sigh not so, but let them go,*
> *   And be you blithe and bonny,*
> *Converting all your sounds of woe*
> *   Into hey nonny nonny."*

"Thanks, Kayla," I said gratefully when she was finished. "I think the Bard pretty much captured where my heart's at tonight."

Zoner stuck a Twinkie into the center of the pit, and we all watched it catch fire. After about ten seconds he withdrew the charred remains and blew on them. Then he stuffed the entire smoking hot confection into his mouth, cried out in muffled pain, frantically reached over to the top of the cooler for the can of chocolate syrup, and quickly alleviated his suffering with one massive swig. "Don't try that at home," he told us after he'd swallowed.

We assured him we wouldn't.

He warmed his hands over the fire and then, rubbing them together with a sidelong glance at Kayla, announced, "Looked up the term *prom* in the old unabridged dictionary this afternoon."

"And what'd you find, professor?" I asked him with a smile.

"A prom is a ball or dance," he intoned, "often given by high school students, see also *anxious,* as a form of self-torture. It's a contraction of the term *promenade,* which means to walk about in a leisurely manner for amusement or show; see also *cruising, posing, hotdogging,* and *avenue-riding.* But to get a real feel for the term, I believe you have to go all the way back to the Latin verb *prominare,* which means to drive a herd of animals forward—see also *high school students.*"

"That's awesome!" I enthused.

Zoner grinned appreciatively. "Etymology rules."

Kayla tossed her copy of Shakespeare over

her shoulder with an exasperated sigh and said to me, "I should just give it up and admit that we're destined to attend the big dance without the benefit of male companionship."

"Hey, don't panic. I might still go, *if* I can find the perfect date," Zoner said.

"Oh *really?* And just what would she be like, pray tell?" Kayla asked.

"Smart, good-humored, easy on the eyes, athletic, and always there for me," he said.

"Oh, terrific," I said, rolling my eyes at Kayla. "Zoner wants to date a Labrador retriever."

We all started laughing and throwing sand at each other.

Kayla spent the night in my guest bed, and per our usual custom, we had a gab session well into the wee hours. Late in the proceedings, she finally confessed the obvious: she'd fallen hard for Zoner. She obviously wanted my support in snagging him, but I found to my surprise that I just couldn't give it to her the way I had to others—Adriana Fernandez, for instance. "You, me, and Zoner make a supremo trio," I said. "And you know as well as I do that if you go after him and it backfires, all three of us could lose out. . . . Besides, I just couldn't risk playing matchmaker here. I'm way too enmeshed as a friend."

"Yeah, I've already thought through all the complications. In fact, I've been obsessing on this subject for weeks. But no matter what I tell myself, Becky, I still love him," Kayla said, using my grade school nickname. "So much that it hurts." Her stressed-out voice resonated in my darkened bedroom.

I'd never loved any guy so much that it *hurt.* In fact, the only guy who'd ever gotten under my skin to that extreme was currently my worst enemy!

It suddenly occurred to me that I might be psychologically bent in some way. I shared my fears with Kayla and told her all about my dynamic duel with Jeff in the *Beacon* classroom, as well as my way dorky trash can impulse.

"Don't stress. If anyone's disturbed, it's Jeff," she said groggily. "He's going out with the queen of the junior class, yet every other column he writes is 'bout you . . . but we're s'posed to be talking 'bout me and Zoner. How d'you s'pose I can get more athletic?"

"Take up skydiving!" I said, suddenly

wide awake. "Are you saying you don't think Jeff is really in love with Darla?" I asked, remembering Eddie's observation that Darla was on Jeff's case a lot these days.

Kayla mumbled something incoherent and then nodded off, apparently for good.

Some people pick the darnedest times to fall asleep.

Chapter 4

PETER CALLED ME about four times an hour on Saturday morning, but he never got any closer to admitting that what he'd done with Cindy was wrong, so I told him he was just tying up the line for nothing and rewarded myself with an Oreo each time I held my ground and hung up on him. When I got a stomachache, I had to stop answering the phone altogether.

Mom went off on Roger when she got home Saturday night and threatened to ground him for a week. I pulled her aside to reason in private. I clued her into the time-tested psychological principle of minimal sufficiency, which holds that mild or moderate punishment is far more likely than extreme measures to reform a delinquent kid. Mom said that it was super unnerving to get parenting tips from a seventeen-year-old, but then she agreed to pare the grounding down to four days, including time already served. After that she tossed back a few aspirin and faded off to slumberland. (She was so stressed that I decided not to keep her up to tell her about Peter and how he'd left me stranded without a prom date.)

Zoner talked Kayla and me into a dawn patrol session on Sunday, but the skies were slate gray and conditions sucked hard, with early onshores and one-to-two-foot slop. It was just as well, though, since I spent most of my time relearning how to paddle and get vertical on my board. Zoner tweaked out a few good rides, and Kayla did her best to match his pace. She bailed more often than not, though, and when Zoner finally razzed her by saying, "You once-a-week surfers don't have a prayer in crumblers like these," Kayla looked totally crushed.

On Monday morning, my arm and leg muscles in agony, I staggered into the PCN trailer to drown myself in other people's woes. As I feared, there was a notable scarcity of boys seeking help, and this was true throughout the day. Jeff's column was basically just a call for a return to "good ol' American self-reliance," after all, and that sort of thing really worked on the male ego. It made me steaming mad, thinking of all those unfortunate guys walking around campus with their problems tightly bottled up inside, just because of Jeff Gardiner's retro-macho attitude.

There were girls in abundance, though. Apparently word of Peter's unfaithfulness had gotten around, and this seemed to boost my popularity with my own gender. (There had to be an easier way!) A lot of the girls who came in just needed to hear the kind of advice I'd recently gotten from Kayla and Zoner, but one case really stood out:

"Walt asked me to the prom three weeks ago," Elaine Stillwell said as she pulled a fresh wad of Kleenex out of the ceramic dispenser (one of my mom's artistic creations; a glossy, cheesy, sunflowery thing that declared: LOVE BEGINS WITH YOU) I kept atop my desk. Elaine's green eyes were bloodshot, her black hair was a tangly mess, and her clothes hung on her like leaves on a dead tree. The poor soul looked as if she'd crawled straight out of bed and into my cubicle. "I was stoked beyond words because I'd been liking him for ages and dropping hints about the prom to him all spring long."

She paused to blow her nose and wipe her eyes again. "We both run cross-country and have the same pre-calc class. He seemed like the nicest guy, and he's *such* a babe—"

"What'd Walt do to get you so upset?" I prompted her. Watching her cry reminded me of how raw I still felt inside, and I was afraid if I didn't keep things moving I might start breaking down myself.

Elaine gave me a sheepish look. "We went out together like six or seven times over the next few months and hung out at school together whenever we could, and things got real intense really fast—the chemistry was just amazing. Even our friends said so. Walt was so gentle and caring, not your typical macho jock at all. He really seemed interested in me as a *person,* you know? Like when I told him about how I want to go into sports medicine someday, he was real enthused for me. He didn't ask me what my GPA was or hammer me with the long odds I faced. And God, I just turned to liquid when he held me in his arms and kissed me. . . ."

Suddenly my lips felt chapped, my throat dry and scratchy. Listening to this sort of thing was a whole lot harder after you'd just suffered a breakup yourself. I decided to follow my counseling instincts and cut to the chase. "So you had sex with him?"

Elaine closed her eyes tightly and nodded. "Last Wednesday, after midnight. In a sleeping bag under that big sycamore tree in Luna Point Park. I was a virgin, so it hurt real bad at first. . . ."

I let her go on describing "it" for a while because she seemed to need to, although by the time she finished I found myself chewing anxiously on a piece of Kleenex as I scribbled notes into my counseling journal. Maybe I should've taken the day off.

"And then within the next few days, Walt dumped you," I heard myself telling Elaine. I'd gone on autopilot, as I once again suffered steamy visions of Peter and Cindy going at it full-throttle in the auditorium balcony. . . .

Elaine's eyes opened wide with surprise. "You mean you *know* already? Has Walt been telling people? I'll *die* of embarrassment!"

I snapped out of my semicomatose state to reach over and take her hand in mine. "Easy, hon. Nobody told me anything. I guessed right only because I've talked to so many girls who've suffered through this same ordeal. And a few guys, too, believe it or not."

We went through the particulars of the breakup, and then Elaine said bitterly, "I feel so stupid and so used! I gave him my virginity, and I'll never get that back."

The Luna Point High School District required sex ed classes in the sixth and ninth grades, in which we were exposed to scads of mind-blowing stats on unwanted teen pregnancies, sexually transmitted diseases, various methods of birth control and their failure rates, and so on. By the time we were sophomores, we were all pretty well-versed. So when students came to *me* to talk sex, the last thing they usually wanted was yet another lecture on "the risks faced by sexually active adolescents." I gave them a pamphlet on the subject instead (the district required it) and then tried to deal one-on-one with the particulars of each case.

"Technically, no, you'll never get your virginity back," I agreed. "You're still master of your own bod, though. Not Walt or anyone else. Elaine Stillwell is in the driver's seat here. And you can decide to have a *second* virginity—"

"But why would Walt do this?" she wailed. "I can't believe he'd use the prom as bait just to score with me!"

Score. Screw. Get laid. Do the dirty deed. Hit a homer. . . . God, I needed some aspirin. "Maybe he did and maybe he didn't. But you'll never get an answer to that question unless you ask him face-to-face, Elaine."

She shook her head. "No *way* I could do that right now!"

"Hear me out first," I urged. I totally understood her feelings, but it was my job to goad her on anyway. "Walt could be lots of things. Maybe he's a creep who'd say anything to get a girl to put out. Or maybe he suffers from a bizarre madonna complex, meaning he loses respect for any female who seems to enjoy sex as much as he does."

Elaine looked totally dragged by these possibilities.

"But on the other hand, what if Walt is a decent guy who really *is* attracted to you as a person and just got so freaked when you connected that he's running scared? If that's the case, who'd you rather talked sense to Walt? His 'typical macho jock' buddies or the girl who loves him?"

"Do you really think I could get him to come back to me?" Elaine asked doubtfully.

"Yo, I didn't say that! First of all, don't think of it as 'getting him to come back.' Among other things, it makes it sound as if you lost him through some fault of your own. Walt's the one who has the explaining to do here, and it's up to you to coax it out of him, gently but *firmly*."

As Elaine thought that over, I took a breather and read through my notes. This was no connect-the-dots sort of case; it was more like a nail-biting nightmare. A girl in her frazzled frame of mind was capable of all kinds of self-destructive behavior, like, for instance, hopping right back into the sack. I could've used a few hours to think this whole thing through, but I'd learned the hard way that the more dire the crisis, the more impatient the counselee. They wanted advice *right now,* or forget it!

"It sounds like you spent your limited time together gabbing about way more than just sex, and I think that's grounds for hope. You don't need me to tell you that lechy boys out for a quick score are almost always zeros on the conversation front."

"You're basically saying this cut-and-run tactic is a universal guy thing?" Elaine wondered miserably.

I shook my head. "On my honor as a peer counselor, generalizations like that are bogus. Think it over. Can you honestly say, for example, that you don't know of any girls who enjoy sex simply for its own sake or of any guys who show loyal, long-term devotion to just one girl?"

"Yeah, I guess I see what you mean," Elaine said. She looked down at the desktop and asked shyly, "Are you still a virgin, Becca?"

Elaine was a junior, and we'd had a few classes together over the years, including, currently, British lit. I liked her well enough, but up 'til now she'd been more or less just a casual acquaintance. So I assumed the sphinx-like expression I practiced in my bathroom mirror for fielding questions like this and said, "Sorry, but that's one I can't answer. It might seem like I was taking sides, and if that impression got around, it might scare even more people away from peer counseling than Jeff Gardiner's managed to."

"You and Gardiner are always nailing each other in the *Beacon*. You totally remind me of Beatrice and Benedick in *Much Ado about Nothing*," Elaine said with a smile.

I let that literary allusion sail by, glad at this point for anything that brought a smile to her face. "I can't answer your personal question, Elaine, but I'd still like to offer you my personal opinion. Three weeks seem like an awfully short prelude to lovemaking, even *with* the prospect of the prom dangling before your eager eyes. I mean, when you think of the risks you're taking—"

"But I told you we were careful!" Elaine interrupted defensively.

"Yeah, *relatively*. But remember Life Skills in ninth grade when Mr. Gerwin showed us all the ways a condom could fail?"

" 'Only abstinence is foolproof, boys and

girls,'" Elaine said, imitating his nasal baritone. We smiled at each other, but then her face fell again. "You think I'm a total sleaze, don't you?" she asked forlornly.

"Not even!" I said, taking both her hands in mine. "All I'm trying to do here is get you thinking *for the future* about protecting your bod from harm . . . starting with your heart. Believe me, Elaine, I know that urge to merge. Virgin or not, I'm just as human as the next girl—"

She finally looked up at me and smiled again. "Yeah, and it's about time! I heard through the grapevine what Peter Karona did to you. Actually, that's sort of why I felt I could come in today. Last week you still seemed like the golden girl who always had her act together, but now that you've actually been screwed over, you seem a little bit more like the rest of us."

I was shocked. "You seriously think I've always got my act together?"

Elaine shrugged. "Practically *everyone* thinks so, Becca. In fact, I'll bet Peter is the first boy who ever got the best of you."

"That's a hoot! Holy smokes, could I tell you stories—," I began, but then I checked myself as I realized I was losing my grip on the session.

"Just tell me one," Elaine pleaded. "Lord knows you can trust me now."

The girl had a point. And we didn't call it *peer* counseling for nothing. "Okay, just one." I rummaged, took a deep breath, and launched in: "The summer I turned thirteen, my family took a vacation in Kauai, and at the hotel I met this sunburned, brown-eyed boy named Lionel from Grand Island, Nebraska. He was the first guy besides my dad to tell me I was pretty, and he made a big deal about my vocab and my swim technique and even the dorky way I ate my meals one course at a time, no matter what."

I hesitated about going on, but Elaine seemed truly enthralled.

"Lionel just generally made me feel so excellent," I continued, "that I was totally willing to overlook his bizarro habits, like the way he wore his T-shirt in the pool and blew bubbles—big bubbles—with his saliva, even in the hotel dining room where the whole world could see. We kissed on Lumahai Beach, where a movie called *South Pacific* had been filmed, and it was so incredibly romantic that I still get the chills whenever I think about it. . . . I even let Lionel put his hand up my top a few times, which felt pretty nice."

Elaine sighed and nodded.

"He got all pouty and quiet, though, whenever I made him stop."

"God, that's so typical!" Elaine said.

"Isn't it, though?"

I was really getting off on the hopelessly naive romance of the tale by this point and actually started to tear up a little. "Lionel and I had this solemn ceremony where we swapped addresses in the moonlight on our last enchanted evening together and vowed eternal devotion to one another. . . . I really *believed* in him—and in us—you know?"

Elaine assured me she knew.

"So like a goof I wrote him a whole slew of letters after I got back to southern California—"

"—and he never wrote back," Elaine concluded sympathetically as she handed me a tissue.

"Not even once." I dabbed at my eyes.

Elaine smiled at me as if she'd just discovered an old friend. "I'll bet you've had your prom dress picked out for months."

"Six," I said, nodding. "You?"

"A year."

We shared a laugh and then talked eagerly about prom stuff for a while, until my next counselee knocked at the door and reminded me of where I was. Embarrassed, I apologized and said, "We'll have this wrapped in just a few."

Elaine got all panicky then and said, "Shoot, Becca, I still have a ton of stuff to ask you! Like what do I say when I talk to Walt?"

I smiled inside. Their meeting was now a given. "First off, let Walt know you're still interested. In him, I mean, not sex." I pondered for a bit and then started to run down a list of his possible motives for bailing on her: "He may've been insecure about his performance; he may've dumped you as a preemptive strike against rejection; he may've decided after the fact that things went too far too fast; or he may think you hate him for 'taking' your virginity, since some guys are still brainwashed to think that way. Whatever the deal is, let Walt know there aren't any hard feelings. And assure him you aren't picking out china patterns—or even trying to find a college you can attend together."

Elaine grinned.

"If he's receptive, ease back into things. Do safe, casual, fun stuff like going out to the movies with a big group of buds. By all means, if he's willing, go to the prom and have a total blast, but pass on the hotel-room scene afterward. And for sure steer clear of those seductive sycamores."

Elaine giggled and then blushed a little. "But what if he isn't receptive?"

"Then you've probably been had, babe, and you'd best cut your losses and move on. Whatever happens, don't let the dude talk you into having sex again as a way of 'making up.' If he takes that line, he's a wolf and good riddance to him. You deserve better. Every girl does."

"Damn, you don't play softball around here, do you?" Elaine said wryly as she slung her backpack over her shoulder and stood up to leave.

I shook my head. "After you've talked to a pregnant sixteen-year-old girl who thought for sure a virgin couldn't make a baby, or you've tried to comfort a seventeen-year-old guy who's in tears over his new STD, 'softball' kind of loses its appeal."

Elaine nodded soberly and then surprised me with a good-bye hug. The gesture left me glowing.

I wished that Becca Singleton, the peer counselor, had been around late last summer at Catalina Island before Becca Singleton, the idiot, decided—after tossing back one too many wine coolers on a moonlit, grassy hillside near a clump of Saint Catherine's lace—to give up her virginity to a slow-handed, sweet-talking eighteen-year-old lifeguard she knew she'd never see again.

Fortunately, I didn't go in for Russian roulette anymore.

Chapter 5

THOUGH HE WASN'T physically there, Jeff Gardiner was very much a presence at the PCN's regular Wednesday afternoon staff meeting.

"Can't anyone force him to stop these attacks? Like the principal?" Ward Yip, a ninth-grade counselor, asked. Ward, who loved number-crunching, had calculated that over the past three days, male patronage of the network was down by about twenty-five percent from the previous week. Female patronage, by contrast, had only declined by about five percent, which was "just on the margin of statistical significance."

"You mean run crying to the administration and play right into the hands of Mr. First Amendment? No way, Ward-o," said Kenyatta Howland, a sophomore counselor. "Let's just go on about our business and pay the paper tiger no mind. The boys'll come back to us eventually, just like before."

"Yeah, but by the time Becca writes her rebuttal and we're back up to speed again, the prom will've passed and the school year will be practically over," Eric Taschner, a senior counselor, pointed out.

"That's exactly what I'm afraid of," I said. "And as you all well know, guys carry just as much baggage about the prom as girls do. The problem is, the *Beacon* only comes out once a month, and I can't see any way around that—"

"Drop in on the J-man," Zoner interrupted.

Everyone looked confused except for Kayla, who nodded and said, "Shoulder hop 'im." Kayla had been standoffish around Zoner since Monday, but at the moment they seemed fully tuned.

"There they go with that surf jive again—," Kenyatta began.

"Translation for the rest of us, please?" Vickie Coolidge, another senior counselor, asked Zoner.

"In most cases," Zoner explained, "it sucks in the extreme to cut in on another surfer when he's already caught a wave. The only exception is—"

"Kooks," Kayla interrupted. "Wave swine."

"Barrel hogs," I said with a smile as I gradually caught on. "But what move do I employ here? A carve? An aerial? A floater?"

"It doesn't matter, just so long as you *show no fear,* Becca," Zoner said, sounding very much like my surfing tutor of three summers ago. "The bottom line is, you don't need Jeff's say-so to get your message across."

"*Now* I'm with you!" Kenyatta said, her caramel-brown face lighting up in a smile. "Let's get the rebuttal out using a different forum. Hell, Zoner, why couldn't you just say that straight-out?"

"Life isn't linear, Kenyatta; it's a *wave* phenomenon," Zoner explained with a grin that only surfers know.

Kenyatta laughed and shook her head.

"How 'bout we do it by posting flyers?" Kayla suggested. "After all, that's how we drummed up business for the network in the first place."

"Of course," I said, getting all excited. "And we plaster the campus with 'em. Especially the hallway near the journalism classroom!"

"Why didn't we think of this before?" Ward wondered.

"I know why," Kayla said, looking directly at Zoner. "Sometimes people get stuck in a trough so deep, *they can't even see what's right in front of their faces.*"

Zoner turned to me. "Kayla's right. You still think too much like a *Beacon* reporter."

Kayla slumped down in her chair. I was kinda worried about her. As if school, counseling, and (above all) the Zoner thing weren't enough, Kayla's mom needed extra help at the family bakery over the next few weeks to replace a vacationing worker. Starting Monday, then, Kayla'd been getting up at five in the morning. When I offered to give her a break a morning or two a week, like I had during the Christmas season, she turned me down cold. Very un-Kaylalike. As I feared, her crush had put our gleesome threesome under siege, and I hadn't a clue what to do about it.

After the group talked over a few hard cases, Zoner, as PCN secretary, took note of referrals made to the regular counseling office during the previous week. "A pregnancy, two suicidals, and a severe drug-abuse case," he reported grimly.

"Those referrals are more important than ever, people," Mr. Gordon, our faculty advisor, said. He wore a crumpled gray derby, a pewter vest over a white Lakers T-shirt, baggy wool dress pants, and a pair of high-top sneakers. This was typical apparel for him; he was a genuine individual. In addition to being a guidance counselor, he taught two psychology classes each term. He liked to joke that "teaching abnormal psych to high school students is like teaching sex to rabbits."

Mr. Gordon always kept a low profile at PCN meetings, so when he spoke up, everybody paid close attention. "Mr. Crampton has been raising a stink at board meetings again about how peer counseling could put the district at risk for liability lawsuits if something went wrong and a parent or student decided to blame one of you. Much as I hate to say it, he does have a point. You've got to be cautious in there. On the other hand, he's also concerned that you may be dispensing advice which encourages, as he puts it, 'rampant sexual promiscuity.' "

Everyone laughed, and then I said, "Mr. Crampton doesn't get it. A lot of our counselees won't talk sex to adults *at all*. Are we supposed to just turn them away?"

"Look on the bright side, Becca. If they take sex off our agenda, you can totally do away with guy counselors," Zoner joked, and everyone laughed again.

Mr. Gordon smiled and said, "You know I fully sympathize here, folks. And as far as I'm concerned, except for abortion-related issues, you can talk sex until the trailer windows steam up, if that's what your counselees need. But be aware that Crampton has started a group called Parents for Total Teen Abstinence, and it's garnering a surprising amount of support in this supposedly laid-back community."

"Parents for Total Teen Abstinence? I don't like the sound of that at all," said Eric Taschner.

"I don't object to the name, per se," I said with a shrug. "After all, if we students have the right to form advocacy groups, it seems only fair to let parents in on the action." Several counselors laughed, but not Eric.

"Only abstinence is foolproof," Herlinda Duarte, a sophomore counselor, shyly but dutifully reminded him.

"And only dweebs quote sex ed teachers," Eric shot back. "I'm not gonna let you or anyone else shove their moral and religious baggage through *my* bedroom door—"

"Hey, *hey!*" I interjected. "Cool your jets, Eric. We're all on the same side here. Sex is a hot topic, for sure, but we've got to try to keep our perspectives, especially with each other."

Eric made a visible effort to calm himself, and then he grudgingly apologized to Herlinda.

Mr. Gordon watched this exchange with obvious discomfort and then gave me a See-what-I-mean? look. "I know many of you are getting questions about sex on prom night," he went on, "and the administration has asked me to remind you of your duty, which you all accepted at the get-go, to warn of the considerable risks and responsibilities involved." He looked directly at Eric. "No matter what, you've got to remember that when you're in that trailer, you're a peer counselor and not an individual advocate for *any* given political or social agenda. If you harbor contempt for the pamphlets you're supposed to hand out when sex comes up, your counselees are going to sense it. We can't afford to be sending mixed messages here. The stakes are way too high." He eased up a bit then and smiled. "But this is just a return to basic training for all you grizzly vets. We all see eye to eye on this, don't we?"

Most of the counselors nodded, but Eric didn't, and he refused to meet Mr. Gordon's conciliatory gaze.

"Are you okay with that, too, Eric?" I gently prompted him. Eric had a short fuse, but he was also an effective counselor, and as a varsity basketball player, he made the PCN "cool" for a lot of other athletes.

"Do you have any idea how many students at this school are sexually active?" Eric asked irritably as he finally looked up at Mr. Gordon.

Mr. Gordon glared back at him, folded his arms across his chest, and looked like he was shifting into heavy-duty lecture mode again.

But then Kenyatta arched an eyebrow and asked Eric, "Taken a bedroom-to-bedroom scientific survey, have you?"

An awkward silence followed, and then after we'd had a few secs to draw a mental picture of that survey-taking process, everyone started to laugh, including Eric and Mr. Gordon. I gave Kenyatta a thumbs-up for finessing away the tension and she beamed.

The meeting was running long by this point, so after rushing through a few remaining procedurals, I wrapped up with the usual reminder to "stay upbeat, listen hard, and don't be afraid to fail." After adjourning I made a point of giving both Eric and Herlinda a reassuring hug and telling each of them how much they meant to the PCN.

Later that night, though, as I was sitting at my computer sweating through the fourth draft of my rebuttal to Jeff's column, Eric phoned in his resignation.

"Having me argue for no sex on prom night," he said, "would be a total, hypocritical sham. There's no way *I'm* abstaining."

I tried for nearly an hour to change his mind about resigning, to persuade him that he had this pegged all wrong. "This isn't a simple case of 'practice what you preach,' Eric," I reassured him in about ten different ways. "If a counselee *brings up* the subject of sex on prom night, Mr. Gordon just wants you to convey that abstinence is the only totally safe option. That's the straight scoop, so no big deal, right?"

There was a long, staticky pause.

"Look, Becca, you've talked my ear off enough for one night," Eric finally said, his voice openly hostile now. "I turned eighteen last month. I'm an adult now. I'm going to *college* in the fall. Do you really expect me to keep pretending that sex is some big deal?"

That's when I had to give in and accept his resignation.

I went to an all-night copy place to print out the flyers and then got Zoner and a few other counselors to come in super early the next morning to help tape and staple 'em up. In the intro to my rebuttal, I hit on a lot of the same points I'd covered with Jeff in our "tennis match" last Friday, as well as some new stuff:

The PCN doesn't exist to assign blame to third parties, as some would have you think. And we know we can't change the fact that this is a messed-up, unfair, and ever-changing world. In reality our main goal is a simple one: to arm you with better coping skills.

What about the stigma of "therapy"? All too often when a person faces a brutal emotional crisis, he is trashed and told scornfully, "Just deal with it; it's all in your head." To show how bogus this kind of reasoning is, imagine for a sec that the same person has just broken his wrist. What would you think of the by-stander who approached the agonized victim with the glib advice, "Just deal with it; it's all in your arm?"

So please remember: talking to us in times of need doesn't mean you're "weak." On the contrary, it just means you're *human*. And happily, so are your peer counselors!

"This rebuttal cranks, Becca," Zoner told me as we posted a few copies on the bulletin board near the entrance to the junior/senior cafeteria. It was just after 6:30 A.M.; the air was cool, the campus was quiet except for the singing of the birds in a nearby oak tree, and the sky was a sort of misty blue. I loved this time of day.

"Thanks, bud," I said gratefully. "You and Kayla really inspired me. And I appreciate your giving up a dawn patrol session to be here for the network."

He shrugged off my thanks with a grin. But after we finished with the board, he turned to me with a look of concern and said, "Becca, are you getting weird vibes from Kayla these days? 'Cause I know I am."

Here it was. The question I'd been dreading. I put on my poker face and said casually, "It's probably just the prom workin' her nerves, you know?"

But Zoner's aquamarine eyes pierced right through my flimsy mask, and he said, "You were verging on a closeout there, Becca, but then you flinched. C'mon, this is the Zoneman you're talking to. Clue me in."

The surfer in me knew that I was riding the lip here, and the slightest mistake could get me pitched over the falls headfirst. I couldn't lie to Zoner, and part of me wanted super badly to help Kayla, but if I told him the flat-out truth and he freaked, our trio could be toast. So I finally said, "She's gone sweet on a guy and wants to go to the prom with him. But he doesn't know it yet, and she's hoping that he'll figure it out on his own." The truth, abridged. The best possible call, I figured, given the dicey circumstances.

"Who's the dude?" Zoner asked.

I tried to read his eyes and thought they betrayed either dread or disappointment. Either way, I was sure he'd caught on, and he wasn't happy about it. (So why was he trying to make me spell it out?!)

"Wait, don't answer that!" he said suddenly, letting me off the hook like the gentle-dude he was. "When Kayla wants me to know details, she'll hip me to them herself."

Killer-smooth roundhouse cutback, Zoner!

We shared a look of relief and then power-shifted to other safer topics as we walked over to the English building in the direction of the journalism classroom. Still, I had to wonder about my next move. Would it be wise to tell Kayla about this nebulous exchange with Zoner or not? I didn't relish the prospect of being the bearer of bad tidings, for sure, but I also didn't want her to go on clinging to what were clearly false hopes.

I felt like I was caught in a riptide off a deserted beach, with no help in sight.

Chapter 6

JEFF GARDINER was already at work in the journalism classroom when we arrived. The room was deserted except for him, and for me it brought back happy memories of early mornings last year, when every so often he and I would pull up news stories on the Internet and play at solving the world's problems.

I was always amazed at how well we got along when there was no one else watching.

"Damn," he said with a half-smile as he smoothed back his platinum blond hair, "when am I gonna learn to keep that door locked? Yesterday morning it was two masked kindergartners with water pistols, demanding my lunch money." He stood up to greet Zoner with an enthusiastic high five. "Can't I wring another surf story out of you, Zoneman? The reading public cries for more! Who can ever forget phrases like 'premium quality shore-pound' or your epic narrative of 'Squirmin' Herman' O'Brien's ride to glory in that 'freak southern hemi tube' that carried him halfway to Laguna Beach?"

"Ease up on the hype, J-man. You embarrass me," Zoner said with a shy grin. He was actually blushing through his tan.

All Jeff's faults aside, when he hosed you with his charm, you felt like a million. He eyed the flyer in my hand a bit uneasily and then asked Zoner, "Whatever happened to Herman, anyway?"

"It turns out that somebody actually caught his miracle carve on video, and the redoubtable Squirmer is now endorsing boards and wowing hoards from Australia to Zuma. And don't josh me, dude. You know why I had to bail on the journalism scene."

"Yeah, yeah, no free time left after peer counseling," Jeff said, his smile waning. "Such a waste."

"Why not do two of your favorite

ex-scribes a little favor," I said, handing Jeff the flyer, "and try reading this piece with an open mind?"

He seized it and read it through with his usual thoroughness and intensity. When he was finished, he gestured at me with the flyer and said, "Not bad. I especially like the broken wrist analogy. But are you implying here that I'm inhuman just because I won't patronize the PCN?"

"Why?" I asked, cheerfully following his logic. "Are you currently in need of help with a personal problem?"

To my surprise his eyes flashed with pain, but he shook his head. "Get real."

Alarmed, I took a step toward him and put my hand on his arm. "Jeff?" I half-whispered, "Is something really wrong?"

He stared at me for a sec, but when he glanced down at my hand, I remembered myself and quickly withdrew it. He abruptly turned away from me and shoved the flyer into the IN box at his computer station. "I'll print this," he said, his voice sounding a bit husky.

"You misread us, J-man," Zoner told him. "We've already put up a hundred copies schoolwide, in places where they'll get max exposure."

Jeff turned back around and said to me, "That's gonna seem a little desperate, don't you think?"

I hadn't thought of it in quite that way and doing so took some of the wind out of my sails, but only for a moment. "That's a risk we're more than willing to take," I said, "considering the high stakes involved."

Jeff grunted. "Yes, God forbid there should be any self-reliant teenagers running loose on this campus." He sounded all too much like his usual contrary self again, and I didn't like it one bit.

"Don't you get it even now?! We want to help people to *become* more self-reliant!" I said, getting angry even though I'd promised myself I wouldn't. "Where'd this idiotic attitude come from? Did you watch too many westerns and action-adventure flicks as a kid and buy into that stupid, megamacho, strong-and-silent-type myth? That's Hollywood, Jeff, not real life!"

"Don't lecture to *me* about reality, Rebecca!" he thundered as he pulled the flyer back out of the IN box, wadded it up, and angrily tossed it into a trash can nearby. He then moved up so close to me that we were practically nose to nose and said, "You don't know a damn thing about my life outside of this school. You haven't a clue!"

My heart was pounding fast now, and it wasn't just from anger. His breath smelled pleasantly of mint toothpaste and his eyes were dazzlingly, intoxicatingly blue, like the ocean on a bright, cloudless day. I had this insane urge to kiss him, but then I remembered Darla. "I don't pretend to know what makes you wig out over the PCN," I said as I took a firm step backward. "And it's true that in all the time I've known you, you've practically never opened up to me about your personal life. But I'm ready to listen now." I'd reclaimed my space; I had the upper hand on the situation again. Now if my heart would just get wise—

"You want me to spill my guts, do you?" Jeff said with a scornful laugh. He turned to Zoner and said, "C'mon, bud, 'fess up. Aren't Becca and most of your fellow counselors just glorified busybodies?"

Zoner tugged thoughtfully on his outrigger canoe earring. "I've never actually seen you two go at each other before," he said. "Kayla's right. There's a definite buzz here."

Jeff and I both started jumping on his case for saying such an outrageous thing, but Zoner just grinned and said, "Methinks you dudes protest too much."

The door flew open wide, Eddie Ballard breezed in, and we all clammed up.

"Back already, Becca?" Eddie asked with a smile. "I thought you drew enough blood last Friday to fatten you up for a month." This was vintage Ballard; he managed to insult you even with his compliments. His gold T-shirt read: IF YOU HAVE TO ASK, YOU CAN'T AFFORD ME. He eyed Zoner uncertainly and then raised his hand in a peace sign and said, "Cowabunga."

Zoner turned to me and asked, "What's he saying? Is that French?"

I laughed and shook my head. Between the obnoxious T-shirt and the way he treated me last Friday, Eddie was fair game for garden-variety teasing. "It's a corruption of *cowadunga*," I explained, "from the Latin *cowadungus horribilis*. In other words, he's telling you you're full of—"

"That's not what I meant!" Eddie protested.

"Etymology—," Zoner began.

"Rules!" I said as we exchanged a high five.

"What's up, Eddie?" Jeff asked as he bit back a smile. "I know you didn't show up this early just to get dumped on."

Zoner and I laughed with surprise, and then Zoner gave Jeff a high five, too.

"It's about the school board meeting you asked me to cover last night," Eddie said, watching us all a bit warily. "It was rather more exciting than usual."

"How so?" Jeff said, sitting down on a desktop and giving Eddie his full attention now.

"Bernard Crampton got hold of the *Party Hearty but Wisely* pamphlet that the prom committee approved for distribution on prom night, and he got quite worked up about it."

"That sounds most alarming," Zoner said, and I elbowed him in the ribs to make him behave. I needed to hear this.

"Crampton thinks the whole Don't Drink and Drive campaign is seen by a lot of teens as an implied *endorsement* of alcohol consumption," Eddie went on. "He didn't get too far with that argument, though, because Cathy Irwin is a member of Mothers Against Drunk Driving, and she buried him in statistics. So then he blasted away at the—and I'm quoting here—'reckless promotion of contraceptives in support of the false and deadly notion of safe sex.' "

"That blows!" I said. "The prom pamphlet was adapted from the one we use at the PCN. Abstinence gets top billing."

Eddie shook his head. "Some reps from PTTA, that's Parents for Total Teen Abstinence, got up to speak, and they said that the pamphlet made it seem as if, quote, 'our kids are *expected* to have sex on prom night.' "

"That logic is hurtin' for certain," Zoner said with disgust. "Are we supposed to believe that if we stop talking about teen sex, it'll die of loneliness? *Not!*"

"How'd things turn out?" Jeff asked. He was furiously scribbling down notes on a yellow legal pad.

Eddie checked his own notes and said, "Crampton's motion to kill the pamphlet failed to carry at first, but the board later reversed itself and, quote, 'agreed to study the matter further' after a lawyer-member of

PTTA got all huffy and insisted, quote, 'abstinence was not given its proper due.' "

"Meaning what?" Jeff wondered.

"There's a district-wide ordinance based on state law," I explained, remembering my PCN training, "requiring all schools to inform students: 'in any forum in which sex-related issues are discussed, that, where intercourse is concerned, abstinence is the *only* entirely safe option.' But the pamphlet does that already, so I still don't see what the big deal is—"

"There's a hidden agenda," Eddie said, one eyebrow arched. "I got the scoop in an interview with Crampton after the meeting."

"Outstanding," Jeff said, slapping his hand down on the desktop. I was impressed, too. Crampton was quite the formidable presence and not easily approached, even by the adult media.

"I was bred to excellence," Eddie exulted, proving once again to be his own worst enemy.

Zoner neighed softly, like a horse. I didn't elbow him this time.

"Crampton's game plan," Eddie went on after a chilly glance at Zoner, "is to get the board to take a strict constructionist stand on the ordinance—that is, to delete references to all options *except* abstinence."

"No way! They'll never go for it," I said confidently. "That'd be a total curb on free speech, and Crampton's already lost that battle once."

"That's just what I was thinking," Jeff said.

"I'm glad," I told him. "I just wish you'd apply the principle more broadly yourself."

Jeff, who never could seem to admit he was wrong or sorry, turned back to Eddie and said, "Good work. This could be very big. I'll go with you to the next board meeting and—"

"Making more plans without telling me, are you, Jeff?" Darla Swanson said testily as she came in the door. I instantly moved several feet farther away from her boyfriend. We all exchanged good mornings and then Darla said, "I just read your flyer and liked it a lot, Becca." She was looking more at Jeff than me, though. "Maybe I'll make an appointment sometime. I'm just loaded with issues these days."

Jeff said to Darla, in an almost pleading way, "You never called me last night."

"Waiting by the phone for a call that never

comes is not a pleasant way to spend your evening, is it, darlin'?" Darla asked sharply as she whipped her long, shimmering dark brown hair over her shoulder.

Wow, I thought, *what goes on here?*

"Time to bail; duty calls," Zoner said, taking me by the arm and guiding my reluctant self out of the classroom.

Eddie followed us out into the hallway and took me aside for a moment. "Do you think Jeff is really proud of me?" he asked with touching eagerness.

"Yes," I said, "and I am too, Eddie. You showed a lot of initiative."

"Thanks," he said, ambushing me with a hug and resting his head on my chest. (He really was short.) I gingerly patted his back and then gently but firmly pulled away. "I didn't want to say this around Jeff," he went on quietly, glancing around as if for spies, "but I think Crampton really has it out for your Peer Counseling Network. He calls it the blind leading the blind, and he's just waiting for one of your counselors to screw up so he can shut you down."

"You can't please everyone," I said distractedly as I took a quick glance back at the open classroom door. You could hear Darla and Jeff yelling at each other now. She was going off about *his parents getting divorced*. I hadn't a clue! That would sure explain the pained look in his eyes. I started to move back toward the classroom, hoping to learn more, when suddenly Zoner appeared in my line of sight, gave me a scowl, and quietly shut the door.

"I think they're on the ropes this time," Eddie told me with undisguised glee. "Darla's turned me down twice for the prom, but the third time might really be the charm in this case."

"I don't want to get involved in gossip," I said, grateful that Zoner was around to keep me on the straight and narrow. Left to my own devices, I'm sure I would've given into my worst instincts and pumped Eddie for more info on Jeff's personal woes.

"Yeah, I can't blame you for being down on gossip these days," Eddie said. "There's probably not a soul left at Luna High who doesn't know about Peter Karona ditching you for a babe-a-licious ninth grader."

I went slack-jawed.

"But don't give up hope," Eddie quickly reassured me. "Santa may have a prom date for you in his stocking yet. Did you wash your hair this morning, by the way? It looks kind of flat . . . unlike the rest of you."

I again removed myself for safety reasons.

As Zoner and I crossed the main quad on our way to the PCN trailer, he went off about Eddie. "I don't see why you even talk to that barracuda. He gives me bad vibes galore. He drops names, makes claims, and plays games. He's as transparent as a jellyfish and every bit as irritating. And he slams you constantly!"

"I know," I said as I fluffed out my hair. "I know. . . . It's just I see these occasional flashes of promise, and I can't help thinking that somewhere deep inside Eddie there's this decent person struggling to get out."

I was starting to feel that way about Jeff Gardiner again, too. . . . In fact, Jeff was practically all I could think about for the rest of the day.

Chapter 7

IT'D BEEN a long week, and late Friday afternoon I left school feeling pretty well whipped. I went home, had a quick dinner, filled the tub with peach-scented bath foam, lit a few candles, and settled in for a good, long soak. I thought about my prom dress, which, after I worked one more shift at the public library tomorrow and picked up my paycheck next Friday, would be mine to wear at last. This led, for no good reason that I could see, directly into yet more thoughts about Jeff Gardiner. Alarmed, I turned quickly to mundane matters and plotted out Sunday, when I planned to catch up on my

French, chem, AP U.S. history, and Brit lit homework. Then I propped my head up on my inflatable bath pillow and decided to clear my mind completely by meditating. I closed my eyes and imagined a seagull flying slowly across a calm, sparkling sea . . . coasting up and down, arcing to and fro, gently, gently. Next, starting with my toes and working up, I imagined that I was relaxing each and every muscle in my bod. . . . Soon I felt a delicious sense of peace and contentment.

My mind drifted. . . . I was at Casino Point on Catalina Island. The lights of the Los Angeles basin were winking at me from across the twenty-five-mile-wide San Pedro Channel. I was wearing my excellent prom dress. Mariah Carey was singing about love. I was in the arms of a handsome stranger in a tuxedo. It wasn't Peter or the lifeguard.

Suddenly the clock tower on the hill above us began to strike twelve. "Kiss me! I have to go back to the mainland!" I said urgently. The stranger took me in his arms and did just that. It was the kind of kiss that was so perfect, so incredibly passionate and heartfelt, it made you want to cry. It tasted pleasantly of mint toothpaste.

"No!" I shouted as I sat bolt upright in the tub. My head was all numb and cottony, and I only gradually realized that I'd overdone the relaxation thing and actually fallen asleep. As I got unsteadily out of the tub, toweled off, and then rubbed on some body lotion, I tried without much success to shake off the weak-kneed feeling of longing the dream had left me with. "Get a grip, girl," I told myself. "It's just a reaction formation." (That's a hostile feeling turned into its exact opposite.) No way it could be a wish fulfillment!

As it turned out, I didn't have much time to obsess over my dream interpretation. A new family crisis flared up later that evening when Mom came home in an extremely cranky mood from a five-hour Ripsnortin' Western Hoedown theme banquet for retired utility execs and opened Roger's third-quarter grade report.

"Roger was never Mr. Honor Roll, but Cs and Ds? Will somebody please tell me how I'm supposed to exorcise the demon that has possessed my child?" she asked with exasperation as she tossed her Stetson aside and began to yank off her gun belt.

I calmed her down with some herbal tea, a

shoulder massage, a few choice tracks from her *Mellow Hits of the '60s* CD, and a plateful of granola bars. I even managed to distract her from waking Roger up for a midnight grill by telling her, finally, about what'd happened with Peter.

"Men are always looking for someone younger!" Mom complained sympathetically. She tended to generalize a lot about men these days. "Do you know your father is dating a thirty-one-year-old now? That cradle-robbing son of a—"

"Mom," I interrupted, taking her hand and putting it against my cheek, "you promised you wouldn't slam Daddy around us."

"Did I, sweetie? I'm sorry," she said as she looked forlornly at her prizewinning coffee table, which she'd fashioned from chain-link fencing and beach trash. She turned and examined my face. "Are you eating your garbanzo beans, honey? If you want to get a prom date on such short notice, you should start by working harder on your skin tone."

"Mother!"

"You're right," she said, throwing up her hands. "Who am I to talk about skin care at the ripe old age of forty-two?" She changed the subject by asking about the PCN and brightened considerably as I brought her up to date. (Mom'd been a psych minor in college and was supportive of the idea from the start.) "That's my girl," she said, putting her arm around me and giving my shoulder a squeeze. "Never step aside for anybody."

But then she smiled in a mysterious way and added, "Of course, in my business we know that free negative advertising can be almost as good in the long run as the expensive positive kind."

"What do you mean?"

"Just think, my little psychologist, about how much attention that 'stubborn and obnoxious' Jeff Gardiner has drawn to your fledgling cause."

This insight made me super uneasy, and I decided it'd be less than wise to tell Mom about my dream.

⌒

Early the next morning I slunk furtively into my little brother's lair to try to prep him for the coming onslaught. I hadn't been allowed to venture into his room for some time, and I was temporarily paralyzed with shock at the scene that confronted me. Convoys of dirty tennis shoes navigated uneasily past islands of unwashed clothes, by way of dingy carpeted straits littered with drifting computer game cartridges and treacherous banks of balled-up Reese's Pieces wrappers. On the walls, toothy, busty, half-naked women leered at me as they posed in positions rarely seen in nature.

Yuck! Was this normal fifteen-year-old guy stuff or did it betray a deeper problem? My instincts tended toward the latter conclusion, even though Mr. Gordon had warned us peer counselors lots of times about "the perils of psychoanalyzing your own family." But how could I help it? Roger was my only sib, and naturally I wanted him to be happy and well adjusted.

I did a quick survey of the titles on his CD rack and concluded that they could be neatly arranged into precisely three categories:

1. Death
2. Sex
3. Death after Sex

There was even a teetering pile of dirty dishes on top of his desk, a molding monument to countless meals eaten in sullen solitude. I was amazed (but also relieved) to find no bugs in evidence. This was apparently the rare sort of environment that even cockroaches shied away from: "No, stay out of *that* room. It could ruin your health."

Saddest of all to me, though, was the fact that his long-neglected electronic keyboard now served only as a dust storage unit.

It seemed to take forever to rouse Roger, and once awake, he was anything but grateful. "So what's the big deal? It's not like I failed anything," he pointed out as he sat up, stretched, and began the scratching thing. I moved to the corner of his bed.

"You got a D in Life Skills, Rog. That's like getting a D in *breathing*."

"I'm enrolled in Life Skills?" he asked with mild surprise as he slipped his Hard Rock Cafe jacket on. At least, I thought with some relief, he didn't actually sleep in the thing.

I continued to stare at him.

"Cut me some slack here, sis," he said. "Isn't one grade grubber in the family enough?"

"I don't grub for my grades!" I protested. "I earn them."

"*Pardonnez-moi,* Saint Rebecca. Of course you do."

I tried to picture the well-groomed, budding musician Roger'd been only two years ago, when Dad was still here in the flesh (to play occasional backup on guitar) and not in the current form of a glossy black leather jacket. "Don't you see how much this hurts Mom?" I asked, trying a different tack.

Something like remorse passed briefly across the apathetic landscape that was my brother's face. But then he jerked a pair of headphones off the nightstand, slipped them over his ears, and used a remote to switch on his stereo system. "Don't you realize how much I don't want to be a little Becca clone?" he shouted, wincing as the sound waves began to assault his eardrums.

Forgetting to grant him any of the patience and courtesy I regularly showed my counselees, I yanked the remote out of his hands, shut off the stereo, pulled off the headphones, grabbed him by the shoulders, looked him straight in the eyes, and said, "That's not what I want, Roger. Look, I *know* it's lousy that Mom has to work all the time, and I *know* it sucks not having Dad around, but I can help you deal, if you'll just *let* me!"

Once again I sensed in him a slight stirring of constructive emotion, a nascent urge to drop the "misunderstood youth" thing and get real at last. But then he drew back and said contemptuously, "My guardian angel. The great peer counselor. Everyone at Luna High thinks you're so bitchin'. But why is it, sis, if you've really got your act so together, that you'll be going to the prom without a date?"

"The *prom?!*" I automatically crossed my arms over my chest, as if all my clothes had quite suddenly fallen off. "My God, Roger, I could care less about the stupid prom right now! I only came into this dump because I'm concerned about *you,* you little—"

I put the brakes on the expletive just in time, pulled out of the skid, and took a moment to try to compose myself. "One of the main reasons you can't play the role of peer counselor with your siblings," I *now* remembered Mr. Gordon saying, "besides the obvious lack of objectivity on your part, is that they often know exactly which of your buttons to push to keep you at bay."

"I apologize for coming into your room un-
invited," I said in a quivering voice as I
scooted back away from him and stood up,
"and I'm sorry for taking such a keen interest
in your welfare. Of course you don't need me
to run interference for you anymore. You're
fifteen now, and you can face Mom—and any
other challenge, for that matter—totally on
your own."

Roger eyed me uncertainly.

I staggered back up the stairs to my own
bedroom and cried buckets over that brutal
crack about the prom.

I'd barely regained my emotional balance
when Peter and Cindy came by the Luna
Point Public Library, where I was doing
my thing as a reference aide and book
stacker. They pretended to browse at mags
and even looked up a few titles on the computer, but I wasn't fooled. I was sure that
Cindy, at least, had come by for one purpose and one purpose only: to stick the knife
called rejection into my back and twist, twist,
twist.

I was on to their game, though, and refused

to be a victim. I remembered Kayla and Zoner's advice and smiled brightly whenever either of them happened to look my way. It actually seemed to make them squirm a bit, *especially* Cindy, which was great (although it didn't seem to be triggering any of those "happy" brain chemicals for me). I kept myself busy reshelving books in the how-to section (which just by coincidence afforded an excellent view of virtually the entire library). I paid absolutely no attention whatsoever to Cindy's tan, slender legs. *How to Get Rid of Unwanted Cellulite.* Or to the too-tight rose pink short-shorts that hugged her perfect little butt. *How to Get a Divorce in California—for Less.* Or to the way Cindy spoke in phony dulcet tones and giggled oh-so-softly at practically everything Peter said. *How to Learn Karate at Home.*

In fact, I eventually lost myself totally in the hypnotic monotony of my brain-numbing work, until—

"Hey, Becca, how are things?"

(Peter's voice. He's right behind me!)

(Betray no emotion. Be strong.)

"Just dandy," I said with elaborate politeness as I turned around to face him. "After all, nobody's betrayed my trust for an entire week."

(Damn. Forgot to play it cool.)

Peter's roly-poly face lost a bit of its color, and he said, "I was hoping we could still be friends."

That one was right up there with "I just got caught up in the moment." I'd given two months of my life to a guy who spouted more clichés than a politician on a campaign trail. "Why not. We're still in chorus together," I said agreeably.

"But you've moved all the way to the front of the soprano section," he complained, "which means I can't talk to you anymore. And the other girls aren't nearly as interesting—"

"Don't dis my choirmates, bud," I said, losing the smile completely.

"Okay, sorry," he said, putting his hands up in a gesture of appeasement. "I'm actually here with some good news. Eddie Ballard's thinking of asking you to the prom!"

"This you call good news?"

"Well, yeah," he said, looking a bit flustered by my less-than-ecstatic response. "I know Eddie can be a little abrasive at times, but he speaks *very* highly of you, and I couldn't stand the thought of you going to the prom alone on account of our little misunderstanding—"

"You mean our misunderstanding who stands about five feet two inches and weighs around a hundred pounds?" I said dryly. "How do you know about Eddie's prom plans, anyway? I don't recall that you two were exactly big-time buds."

Peter nodded. "True enough. But Sergio Hernandez threw one of his famous fiestas down at the beach last night. Eddie got kinda wasted, as usual, and before Serge finally gave him the ol' boot, Eddie got to bragging about his prom list."

"Prom list?" (ALL HANDS ON DECK! INSENSITIVE MALE SIGHTED OFF THE STARBOARD QUARTER!)

"Yeah," Peter said with a big smile, "a list of his top ten choices for prom dates. I'll tell ya, that guy has guts, carrying on the way he does. Anyway, the first seven girls turned him down 'cause they'd already committed. That's what they told him, anyway. And so after he hits up number one for the third and last time, he . . ."

(ALL HANDS TO BATTLE STATIONS! THIS IS NOT A DRILL!)

Peter paused for a moment. "Is there something wrong? Why are the corners of your mouth twitching that way?"

"If you have to ask," I said through clenched teeth as I pulled an appropriate title off the shelf, "I can't explain it."

Peter shrugged and went blithely onward. "So the way I figure it, Eddie'll be approaching you soon," he said with an encouraging smile, "because you're number—"

(FIRE ONE!)

As I began to take a swing at Peter with the hardcover book *What Men Should Know about Women,* he took a step backward, tripped on his own shoelace, and fell to the floor.

The next few minutes were sort of a blur. Cindy, who'd heard Peter fall, came running over from another part of the library, screamed, showered him with kisses, and then, with my shamefaced assistance, helped him to a chair.

Ms. Lopez, the reference librarian, rushed over and asked if Peter needed medical attention.

"No, no, I'll be okay," he insisted.

"Rebecca," Ms. Lopez said sternly, "what happened here?"

I opened my mouth to speak, but no words came forth. After all, what could I say? I knew perfectly well it was totally against library policy to try to club a patron with a book. (And I also knew that I'd watched *way* too many navy war movies as a kid, although doing so'd allowed me to spend major quality time with my dad.)

"I, uh, tripped—and fell," Peter finally said as he carefully avoided looking at me.

I know it's irrational, but I hated him even more for being so gracious about it.

Cindy leaped into his lap and got all cooey and clingy.

The sleaze.

"Tripped over *what,* young man?!" Ms. Lopez asked, more alarmed than ever. Her eyes quickly scanned the area where Peter'd fallen and apparently detected no obstructions. Then she turned around for just an instant to glance at the library entrance, no doubt expecting an army of attorneys to come streaming in at any moment.

"My shoelace," he said sheepishly as Ms. Lopez turned back to face him.

Ms. Lopez's features relaxed at once, and she expertly shifted gears into a quick, informative minilecture about shoelace safety. Before she could take questions, though, she was called back to her desk. It was just as well, because as far as I could tell, Peter and Cindy'd tuned Ms. Lopez out long ago as they lapsed into the notorious teen-couple-oblivious-to-the-existence-of-all-other-life-on-earth mode.

"Is my Pedew Wabbit all beddew?" Cindy asked in a singsongy, childlike voice as she continued to plant kisses on his head.

"Yeth, Thumperkins," he replied in a similar sort of voice. Then they twitched their noses at each other and shared a kiss on the lips.

Deliver me, Lord! I'd been planning to apologize to Peter, really I had, but witnessing this depressingly intimate and unself-conscious exchange had totally robbed me of the impulse.

Peter'd never called *me* by a pet name.

Peter'd never kissed *me* in a public place.

"I'm glad you're okay, Peter," I finally forced myself to mutter.

He turned reluctantly away from "Thumperkins," gave me a sharp, mistrustful look, and said, "Yeah, it's a good thing you're always around when I fall."

"C'mon, let's ditch this place," Cindy said as she glared at me and put a possessive arm around her boyfriend. "It's just full of creepy hazards today."

"Out of the frying pan, Cindy dear," I said as I looked directly at Peter, "and into the fire."

Cindy didn't seem to get it, but I knew she eventually would, one way or another.

Chapter 8

KAYLA SURPRISED ME when she came by near the end of my shift at the library and asked me if I wanted to go surfing. I actually preferred to carve in the early morning, before the afternoon onshore breeze began to howl, but after my sorry showing last Sunday, I figured I needed all the water time I could snag. Besides, we'd gone all week without a single good talk, and I was missing her intensely.

I had only two boards in my quiver, and I picked the longer, heavier one (seven feet four inches), dubbed Moby Dick for its girth and off-white color, because I was still feeling rusty and unsure of myself. When I caught up with Kayla at her house, though, she surprised me again by introducing her brand-new neon rainbow-colored stick, a six-foot ultralight missile that was ready to soar. Kayla stands just over five feet herself (not counting the inches added by her Pebbles Flintstone 'do), and she has powerful legs, but I still thought this was a bold investment.

"What goes on?" I asked after we had the boards secured to her roof rack and were motoring to the beach. "Won't this bust your prom budget?"

"I've decided to make my own dress," Kayla said with a mysterious smile. "I think it's great you're going the expensive lace/ puffed sleeves/brocade route, Becca, but for me, this board is a better investment over the long haul."

As we shed our street clothes and waxed up our sticks on the beach, I complimented Kayla on her new black bikini and then told her about Peter's visit to the library and why I ended up trying to deck him. "Imagine what my counselees'd think if they found out how I handled *that* particular confrontation," I said guiltily.

"Give yourself a break. Once we start

expecting perfection of ourselves just because we're peer counselors, it's time to throw in the towel," she said. While we were both bending over to strap on our ankle leashes, she added, "Besides, your counselees think you're pretty hot. Just yesterday in my Spanish class, Adriana Fernandez was singing your praises for advising her on how to find out if her guy friend Omri might be ready for a more serious relationship. Seems he's rather keen on the idea. Could be a prom date in their future."

"Hey, Kayla, I'm really sorry—," I began as I stood back up and straightened out my gold-colored one-piece (I'd found out the hard way that when I'm in the surf, a bikini top and I are soon parted).

"Don't sweat it," she said as she picked up her board and flashed me a reassuring smile. "You hipped me to your stance on the Zoner issue already, and I totally respect it. Besides, I'm beginning to think I've got this wired all on my own."

As we started down for the water, I heard a familiar voice yell out teasingly, "Hey, I didn't know chicks could surf! I thought they only sat on the beach and watched!"

It was the Zoneman himself, already out in

the lineup. "Did you know he was down here?" I asked Kayla. It wasn't a trivial question, 'cause he frequented a whole range of breaks between Trestles and Seal Beach, especially on weekends.

"Can chicks surf?" she replied in an aggro tone as she charged the white water, slipped onto her new board, and began to paddle out.

The waves were breaking two to four with decent shape, and while the westerly was a presence, it was certainly no blowout. The ocean sparkled; the crowd was casual. I was still shaky in the clutch, but I wasn't wiping out nearly as much as last weekend. I was remembering how to ride the waves, instead of letting them ride me. And as luck would have it, I got one four-footer all to myself. I caught the slot, crouched low, and let my instincts take over. For the first time in months my mind was truly freed of static, and I remembered why I got into surfing in the first place. It wasn't just because it was the sport of choice for Nobel Prize winners like Donald Cram and Kary Mullis—surfing had *soul*. Totally pumped up with confidence, I carved my way up to the lip, slammed it, did my one tail slide of the day, and cut back down to the trough again. I could hear other surfers, especially Zoner and Kayla, hooting their encouragement. And then I lost control of the wave and ate it. It was a routine wipeout, though; I took some water up the nose, went with the flow, and came up laughing and happy. Wipeouts, like long waits between ridable sets, come with the territory for everyone who surfs, be they grommet or world champ. The sport is nicely humbling and democratic that way.

Kayla, though, was doing an impressive job of keeping her wipeouts to a relative minimum. She'd always been what Zoner called a natural talent, but I'd never seen her go for broke like this before. She ripped, she shredded, she slashed. She did tail slides, she did aerials, she slammed into overdrive and paaaartied! It was quite the riveting spectacle.

"You were awesome out there today, Kayla!" Zoner enthused when we all returned to the beach more than an hour later. He examined her board and said, "This is a fine design, but there's more to the rad moves you pulled off this afternoon than any new stick can account for. What gives?"

Kayla gave him the same mysterious smile

she'd flashed at me earlier and said, " 'Natural talent,' remember?" He watched her with more than casual interest as she toweled off, and he laughed like a little boy when she shook her wet reddish blond mop at him. He swallowed hard, though, when he noticed I was watching him. Did he feel put on the spot by her flirting, or was he enjoying it? I couldn't totally tell, but I figured if he *did* have the hots for her, he'd've told me on Thursday morning.

"Word's out there's a storm off Baja, which means we could have a killer swell coming in early next week," Zoner said. "You girls interested?"

We both were.

"You'll want to play it cautious in the big waves, though, Kayla," he said with concern. "The risks are way higher."

"No fear," she said playfully as she cast her towel aside, thrust her chest out, put her hands on her hips, and struck a defiant pose.

Zoner swallowed hard again. Twice.

Just then Barney "Barn Burner" Manaba came thundering up the beach from the water, hefting his surfboard under one of his enormous arms as if it were nothing more than an oversize clipboard. After greeting us girls and congratulating Kayla on her "epic session," he said to Zoner, "Look, brah, Sabrina needs to know pronto if you're gonna take her cousin Brandi to the prom or not. Brandi's losing her patience; it's not like she's hard up for a date."

Zoner grinned sheepishly at us, punched Barney on the shoulder, and said, "This is neither the time nor the place, dude. I'll buzz ya later."

"You better," Barney said. Then he winked at me and thundered up the beach toward the parking lot. What was the wink for?

"I was only hipped to Brandi's interest in me last week," Zoner explained without our needing to ask, "and I was too embarrassed to tell you guys about it. Truth be told, I've had yet another prom invite since then. With all the good vibes coming my way, I'm starting to think that spending Saturday night in the grand ballroom of the Luna Point Sheraton wouldn't be such a gruesome ordeal after all."

So he was already considering not one but *two* prom invites! Poor Kayla would just have to face facts. The dude was obviously not interested in her as anything more than a—

"Good for you," Kayla said, walking over to Zoner and giving him a hug. "But don't let yourself get pressured into making a choice you'll regret later. Most dances you'll forget, but word is, prom memories can last a lifetime. C'mon, Becca," she said, turning back to me. "Let's go, get changed, and have dinner at the mall. My treat. I'd invite Zoner along, too, but he has to speed home and make an important phone call."

As I picked up my backpack and my board, Zoner gave me a questioning look. I shrugged and gave him a tentative thumbs-up. Who'd've thought Kayla would take this so well?

The Luna Point Mall had your basic food court: shiny tile floor, two illuminated fountains, a sea of white wrought-iron tables with matching chairs, a glass ceiling highlighted around the edges by swirling red, green, blue, and yellow neon tubes. It featured about a dozen fast-food outlets, offering the fresh, the fried, the filleted, and the floundering. Lots of dessert options, too, but for me there was only the frozen yogurt stand. I was especially partial to the nonfat Alpine white chocolate with—

"Becca, I know something's bothering you," Kayla said.

—with carob sprinkles, or, when they were out of that, the passion peach with fresh strawberry slices was a reasonably orgasmic substitute.

"Why do you keep saying that?" I asked irritably.

"Because you're jabbing your egg roll with a fork and stirring your chicken chow mein around. When you're upset you always tease your food instead of eating it. It's like you're testing it for character flaws."

I dropped my fork as if it'd betrayed my confidence. "Okay, Kayla, you're right. I can't for the life of me figure out how your surfing improved so much between last Sunday and today."

Kayla averted her eyes and took a humongous bite out of her tuna-pineapple-walnut-and-alfalfa-sprout sandwich from Flaky Frank's Bagel Blitz. I knew she was buying herself time to think. Once she'd swallowed, she took a long drag of her mango smoothie and then said, "I told you a little white lie because you said you didn't want to be involved."

"Involved in what?" I asked as I picked up my fork and began poking at my food again.

"Zoner, of course! I told you I had to work at the bakery for the next couple of weeks, but in fact, with my mom's okay, I've been heading up to Westport Beach every morning at five to practice my surfing. I happen to know Zoner avoids that break 'cause he got hassled badly there as a grommet. But as you saw, it's been doing wonders for me."

I was aghast. "How could you lie to me, Kayla?! I just told Peter this morning that I'd gone a whole week without someone betraying my trust, and now I find out—"

"Hey, I'm really sorry," she said, getting up from the chair across from me and moving into the one next to me. "I hadn't thought of this in terms of the Peter thing at all. But of course you can trust me, Becky. I'm your best bud." She patted my arm reassuringly and waited patiently for me to make eye contact so I could see for myself that she was being sincere.

Her manner was so caring and classically PCN that, in spite of my disappointment, I had to fight an urge to smile. "Promise me you won't do that again," I asked her. "Tell me a lie, I mean. White or not."

"Are you sure?" she asked skeptically.

I nodded.

"Okay," she said, "here goes. Your surfing stance needs major work; you stress too much over Roger; I never understood what you saw in Peter—you should've gone for Jeff Gardiner last year when you still had both the inclination *and* the opportunity—"

"Stop!" I said with a laugh, putting my hands up. "I think I get the point. . . . But you see mine, too, right?"

Kayla nodded, we exchanged a high five, and she pulled her bagel over to continue munching. I started to eat at last myself and discovered that doing so quickly chased away the dizzy headachy feeling I'd had for the last hour or so.

"Are you sorry you bought the board now, since things didn't work out the way you hoped?" I ventured to ask her a few minutes later.

"What do you mean? Things are going

great!" Kayla said brightly. "I've shown a deepening interest in something Zoner cares loads about, but I've also managed to pull back from him a bit as a friend—you know, to create some mystery."

"But what about the potential prom dates he mentioned?" I asked, amazed that she could still be so optimistic.

Kayla gave a dismissive wave. "No commitments have been made. And didn't you see the signs this afternoon? Zoner was swallowing like mad, and his pupils were dilating. He's clearly dealing with some heavy-duty emotions when I'm around."

"But what if they're not the emotions you think—," I began to say, when suddenly we were interrupted by a loud SMASH!

It came from a table over near the McDonald's. We turned and saw Chris Bowen and some other kid laughing like Beavis and Butt-head as they crushed Happy Meal toys with their fists.

"I thought Chris Bowen was in jail," Kayla said.

I froze suddenly as I realized that Chris's companion, whose back was to me, was wearing a black leather jacket with the Hard Rock

Cafe emblem on the back. His hair was shaved on the sides and black at the top.

I counted to ten. Three times. I did my deep-breathing exercises. I thought through the confrontation *before* it happened. "That's Roger with him, isn't it?" Kayla asked with a sympathetic look as she watched me do the breathing thing.

I nodded. I'd told her earlier about what happened—or rather, didn't happen—that morning.

I stood up and calmly walked over to their table. I came up behind Roger, and Mitch's eyes went wide as he announced, "It's your sister!" in much the same way he might've said, "It's a T rex!"

Roger's arm froze in midstrike, just inches above a soon-to-be-smashed plastic movie pro- motion cup. ("A limited time offer, available only at participating locations. Collect all four while supplies last!") I pulled up a chair be- side his, put my arm around him, and said calmly, "Roger, it may've slipped your mind, but you're supposed to be at home right now, catching up on your schoolwork."

The mention of the word *schoolwork* caused Chris to flinch. He slipped on a pair of aviator sunglasses and began to knead his fully shaved head like bread dough.

"Nobody on the planet would be caught dead doing homework on a Saturday night, not even you," Roger said without looking at me.

Chris grinned. (I would reflect later that the absolute worst thing you can do to a fifteen-year-old boy is humiliate him in front of some older guy he is trying desperately to impress.)

"All the same, I'm taking you home," I said, still calm.

"In your dreams, Sister Do-Right."

Chris was smiling now.

"You're cruisin' for trouble, mister!" I said, starting to lose it.

"I'm paralyzed with fear," he said, shaking my arm off his back. "Look, Becca, do us *both* a favor and drop the mommy act. If I needed a parent, I'd have one at home."

The outburst of laughter from Chris shot through me like a flaming arrow. "We'll discuss this further in the car," I said as I stood up and took him by the hand.

"That's no *car*. That's a dumpster with windows!" he said as he stood up and yanked his hand away from mine.

Chris laughed even louder this time, and Roger beamed triumphantly.

"You don't want to make a scene here, Becca," Kayla gently advised me from the sidelines. "Let it be."

I couldn't. At that particular moment I was convinced I was the only remaining boundary in Roger's life, and I knew from my study of psych that we all *need* boundaries to feel loved. So I came up behind his back, laced my arms around him, clutched a hand on each side of the open front of his jacket, and vowed to hold on no matter what. "Please come home with me," I said.

"Have you flipped?" he said, beginning to squirm. "Let go of me!"

"Why've you become so determined to trash your life?" I said as I struggled to hang on (he was a whole lot stronger now than when we used to roughhouse as kids). "Don't you care about anything anymore?"

"Noooooo!" Roger declared in a loud, primal yell that choked back a sob. Then he elbowed me square in the ribs, tore himself loose, and bolted.

Chapter 9

I STAGGERED IN through the back door of my apartment with Kayla's aid and plotzed into a chair at the kitchen table. There was a note stuck to the chartreuse ceramic napkin holder; Mom had gone to an art film entitled *Winter in Helsinki* with someone named Ulrich, and before leaving, she'd given Roger "permission to watch TV after three hours of studying." At the bottom of the note she'd scrawled, "P.S. *Please* don't wait up for me!"

Mom always freaked when I burned the midnight oil for her. "Becca, you're seventeen going on fifty," she'd say. But who else was going to wait up and make sure the woman got home safely?

I unbuttoned my blouse and felt around my rib cage. No breaks, but there was certain to be a major bruise by tomorrow.

Kayla opened the freezer, located the ice tray, and pulled out a handful of cubes; she put them into a Ziploc bag, wrapped the bag in a hand towel, and then handed me the first-aid package.

"You're a saint," I said thankfully as I gently pressed the pack against the point of impact. Oh my *God* that hurt!

"Where do you suppose Roger is now?" Kayla asked after closing the freezer.

I shook my head. "I haven't the foggiest, although I suppose he might be casing out a Catholic church somewhere, hoping to take down a few nuns while the night is still young."

Kayla laughed. "C'mon, Becca, you were riding the poor kid. Literally."

"I know," I said with a sigh. "Mr. Gordon thinks I'm in danger of developing a savior complex. It's a hazard that all counselors face, he says. But I don't see how I can stand idly by while Roger makes a mess of his whole life—"

"It could just be a stage," Kayla said. "He may grow out of it."

"Then how come most of the ninth-grade boys at Luna High aren't getting into such dire straits?"

"You've got a point," she admitted. "So let's look at another possibility. The really bad stuff—the vandalism, the talking back to teachers and giving them unsolicited haircuts, the plummeting grades; that all didn't start until about midyear, did it?"

I had to think about it. "No, I guess not, now that you mention it. It was definitely after we'd gotten the PCN started." I suddenly caught on to what Kayla was driving at and didn't like it one bit. "You don't think he's acting out because of jealousy, do you?"

Kayla shrugged and said, "I've been amazed at the harsh feelings some of my counselees have for their star sibs. After all, it's a drag to go through high school in someone else's shadow."

Roger's question—"Don't you realize how much I don't want to be a little Becca clone?"—suddenly echoed in my mind, right along with "Everyone at Luna High thinks you're so bitchin'."

"Am I supposed to shift into low gear just so my kid brother won't feel like a failure?"

Kayla shook her head. "I'm not saying Roger's resentment of you is *rational,* Becca. I'm just trying to help you get a sense of where his mind is at."

Just then the phone rang, and I shook my head when Kayla motioned whether to pick it up. "Let's see first if it's important," I said. I was half-afraid it'd be Peter (one of his virtues was that he never stayed mad at anyone for long) with a hot new lead on a prom date, and I just couldn't deal right now. After four rings the answering machine came on:

"Hi, you have reached the Singleton residence," Roger's voice said. *"Roger is out charming the babes; Heidi is either at work or on a date with yet another loser; and Becca is out minding other people's business. Please leave a message, and one of us will get back to you when we damn well feel like it. Thank you."*

"I can't believe that little creep hijacked the answering machine *again!*"

Kayla nodded sympathetically and bit down on a smile.

"Uh, right-o," the message began. "This is for Becca, from Eddie. I hope you're sitting down when you hear this! After weeks of excruciating deliberation, I've decided to make *you* my prom queen!"

Long, dramatic pause.

"No, it's *not* too good to be true! I'm on the up-and-up here. Darla's loss is your gain! I know you've been hard up for a prom date ever since Peter was caught learning ninth-grade geography the hands-on way but despair no more. He should've recognized that a girl with your intelligence and integrity would not tolerate such a lustful indiscretion! Rest assured that when my limo pulls up at your humble doorstep on May fourteenth, you'll be entering the rarefied company of a guy who has only the highest esteem for your many breasttaking qualities. So call back ASAP to confirm, and I'll take care of the rest. (He left his phone number.) Bye for now, Rebecca darling."

Beep.

"Did he really say *breast*taking?" I asked.

We replayed the message just to make sure.

"Methinks that's what they call a Freudian slip, 'Rebecca darling,' " Kayla said as we both began to howl with laughter.

"And to think I told Zoner just the other day that I still had hope for this guy," I said, shaking my head in disbelief.

Kayla stuck her hand up into my face and said, in Eddie's faux aristocratic drawl, "Kissss my rrrring, peasant!"

"Uh, right-o," I said, giving Kayla's hand a doggie lick. Then I cupped my hand to my ear and said, "But forsooth, methinks my most esteemed gentleman beckons even now!"

"You'd breast be off, then!"

The two of us laughed until we both had tears in our eyes.

Later, after I'd tossed my blouse into the hamper and changed into a comfy terry cloth bathrobe, we brewed a pot of apple-cinnamon tea and used it to chase down some Oreo cookies as we brainstormed for a fitting response to Eddie's odious overture. The idea came to me in the middle of my third Oreo. . . .

"So it's yes, then," Eddie crooned with supreme confidence after we'd exchanged greetings.

"Well, not exactly," I said apologetically. "You see I . . . It's just that . . . Oh, this is *ever* so awkward!"

Kayla, listening on a phone that she'd brought in from the living room, gave me an encouraging thumbs-up.

"You're not playing hard to get, are you?" Eddie asked with obvious disbelief.

I almost went off on him right then, but Kayla shook her head and held up her free hand in a calming gesture.

"Heavens no," I managed to say with alarm. "In fact, I was so overcome with emotion when I first heard your message that I actually felt *faint*."

"Ah, well, that's understandable—"

"And rest assured that if it wasn't for this wretched list, I'd accept your gracious invitation on the spot!"

There was a very long pause, during which Kayla and I exchanged triumphant smiles.

"What kind of, er . . . 'list' would that be, exactly?" Eddie asked.

"Well, it's— God, Eddie, I'm so embarrassed to admit this; you're going to think I'm an absolute slug or something—it's a *prom* list. A rank-order roster of the ten guys I was considering as potential prom dates. And you see, the *really* awkward thing here is, I haven't gotten all the way down to your name just yet. I feel rotten about it, but there you are."

There was an even longer pause this time.

I drew a line across my neck with my index finger, and then Kayla pantomimed an elaborate, blue-blooded swoon to my silent but enthusiastic applause.

"Becca," Eddie said, his voice all crackly and indistinct now, like the dying signal from a distant radio station, "I don't know exactly what you've heard, but I'm sure if you'll just let me explain—"

"WRITE IT ON A CARD AND SELL IT TO HALLMARK, YOU JERK!" I raged, dropping the act completely. "I'd rather walk naked into a biker bar to talk sexual harassment than go to the prom with the likes of you! Good night and good riddance, you human oil slick!"

As I slammed the phone down, Kayla

crowed, "He's toast!" and we exchanged a triumphant high five.

An hour or so later, as I struggled to keep my worries about Roger in check and tried to calm my nerves with a generous serving of nonfat chunky peach sorbet, Kayla asked me why I was so pessimistic about her prospects for getting to the prom with Zoner. I finally told her about Thursday morning, when I'd indirectly hipped Zoner to her intent and he had seemed less than jazzed by the prospect of Kayla-as-girlfriend.

"But your reading of his reaction—that's pure speculation on your part," Kayla said after downing a spoonful of nonfat raspberry frozen yogurt. "Why make it sound conclusive?"

Frustrated, I laid out all the evidence for her one more time and said, "Maybe I'm wrong, but I just can't shake the feeling that you're setting yourself up for a big disappointment."

Kayla looked doubtful for the first time. She scooped out another bite of frozen yogurt and took her time about swallowing it. Finally she said, "Do you remember a few years ago at summer surf camp when Zoner told us not to dread wipeouts 'because if you're not wiping out, it means you're not going for broke and testing your limits'?"

I nodded, not sure what she was getting at.

"Well, maybe I am kidding myself and Zoner *doesn't* see me as anything more than a bud, and maybe my going after him in such an aggro way *will* screw up things for the three of us, although I don't really see how my friendship with you or your friendship with him will be hurt. The bottom line is, though, I'm fully willing to risk 'wiping out' here, if that's where things are headed. So be a friend and let me, okay?"

"If that's what you really want," I said reluctantly. "But I hope you'll take what Zoner said this afternoon seriously. You gotta be careful not to get in over your head if it really pumps next week."

"No worries, girl," Kayla said with a reassuring smile. "I have a Zoner wish, not a death wish."

I started to get *really* anxious about Roger when eleven o'clock came and went, but Kayla suggested I wait a 'little while longer' before firing up the Olds and embarking on a search-

and-rescue mission. To burn off some nervous energy (and Oreos), we closed the shades in the living room, stripped down to our underwear, popped a dance video into the VCR, and began to jam. Kayla did, anyway. I mainly held a fresh ice pack against my rib cage and paced like a lioness in a third-rate zoo.

"Kayla, what makes you think I wanted to go for Jeff Gardiner last year?" I asked after about sixteen passes around the coffee table.

Kayla blew a sweaty strand of hair out of her eyes and, without looking away from the TV or slowing her amazin' pace, said, "It was totally obvious. You never admitted to a crush, but you talked about him constantly. Not that *that's* changed. And anyone with half a brain can see you and Jeff make a natural pair . . . like salsa and chips, Goobers and Raisinets, or even Fred and Wilma."

I finally tossed my ice pack onto the table, kicked back on the couch, and said, "You lie. We've got practically nothing in common."

"I tell the truth," Kayla countered as she continued to make like Janet Jackson at a dance contest. "You and Jeff are both fiercely proud, superstubborn, megadriven—"

There was a sound of a key entering the

lock in the front door, and Kayla broke stride, whipped her clothes off the rocking chair, and disappeared from the room at lightning speed. I switched off the TV and had my bathrobe barely half on when the door opened and Roger came in.

His eyes went straight to my torso, and he winced when he saw the forming bruise.

I looked him over, too, and saw a scraped forehead, a swollen lip, and no Hard Rock Cafe jacket.

"My God, Roger, what happened?!" I asked as I finished putting on my robe.

"I'm sorry I hit you, Becky," he said, his eyes glistening. "I really am."

"Don't worry about that," I said, though I was extremely grateful and not a little surprised to hear those words come out of his mouth. "Please tell me what happened!"

"I was screwing around. I found some buds to hang with after I left the mall, and just for the hell of it, we went hopping fences down at the marina. I got snagged on that really high one around the storage area at the Luna Point Yacht Club and ended up tearing the jacket practically in half. Then I fell about eight feet and landed wrong."

He made minimal eye contact with me, especially when he was talking about the jacket, and the story came out sounding way too smooth and well rehearsed. He was almost for sure lying, at least in part.

"Why didn't you bring the jacket home?"

"I wasn't going to stay at the mall for very long," he said, totally shifting gears as he looked directly at me now. "You didn't have to make a federal case out of it!" A renegade tear escaped from his right eye, and he immediately wiped it away with the back of his hand.

"I'm sorry for going overboard," I said, feeling rotten.

"Prove it," he said. "Don't say a word about this to Mom or anybody else. She'll just figure I stopped wearing the jacket and jump for joy. It was from Dad, after all."

Unfortunately, Roger had Mom pegged perfectly on this one. "Okay," I agreed, "but first please tell me what *really* happened to you after you left the mall."

"Good night, my loving, ever-trusting sister," he said disgustedly as he turned away and started to walk toward his room. "It's been real, as always."

At a total loss for words, I sat back down on the couch, closed my eyes, and imagined I was surfing.

Kayla popped back into the living room a few minutes later, fully clothed and with a freshly washed face. "I heard Roger's voice," she said in an excited half-whisper. "Is he okay? Did you guys work things out already?"

"He's one hundred percent himself. And yeah, we swapped apologies," I said as cheerfully as I could.

"That's awesome," Kayla enthused, clapping her hands together. "Like they say, the darkest hour is just before dawn."

But I couldn't shake this terrible feeling that the "darkest hour" was yet to come.

Chapter 10

By MONDAY AFTERNOON when two guys in a row came in to see me for counseling, I knew for sure that my rebuttal to Jeff's column was having some major impact on its target audience.

"No crisis too small, right?" Denny Chan asked. He was staring at me intensely over the round, silver, wire rims of his glasses. He had an open notebook in his lap and a pen at the ready.

"You bet," I said.

"Okay, here's the deal," he said, pointing the pen at me. "I've asked Kristen Stern to the prom and it's a go, but I'm a little worried about . . ."

There was a long pause here, as Denny worked his jaw muscles and pulled at the sleeves of his black wool blazer, which he was wearing over a faded football jersey.

From experience I knew that these long guy pauses meant I was supposed to guess at the problem, so after a minute or two'd passed, I started ticking off possibilities on my fingertips. "You're a little worried about: the cost, looking like a dork in a cummerbund, gabbing with her friends, dancing, kissing—"

"*That's* it!" he said, snapping his fingers and looking relieved. "Thing is, Kristen and I haven't actually . . ."

". . . kissed yet," I ventured.

He nodded again. "And to tell you the truth, I've had some problems in that area. This one girl I went out with said I French-kissed like a Saint Bernard, although I've wondered ever since how she would know that. So I changed my technique, and the next girl I kissed said if she wanted her mouth examined, she'd go to a dentist. Help me out here, Becca. What am I doing wrong?"

I'd gotten this kind of question lots of times, from both guys and girls, so I felt reasonably confident about handling it. I assured him first off that kissing was a mystery for *everyone* and that tastes (so to speak) varied a lot from person to person. "It sounds like in the first case you might've gone a little overboard on the saliva thing, and in the second, there was maybe too much tongue action on your part . . . although I think the way your kissing partners slammed you was totally uncool."

Denny looked up from his notepad and smiled appreciatively.

I'd had my share of loser kissing experiences, so I knew how dragged he must've been feeling about himself. "Next time," I went on, "depressurize by taking a follow-the-leader approach, at least until you and your partner've gotten to know each other better. In other words, let her show you what works for her first, and then gradually phase in what works for you. If the vibe is right in the rest of your relationship, you'll eventually reach a good space in your kissing, too. Don't be shy about asking her for make-out tips, either— most people love to play teacher, and besides, modesty is sexy."

Denny checked over his notes carefully. "This looks real. I can handle this," he said confidently. "And I assume from what you've said that this business of people being kiss-compatible from the start is just one of your basic myths, right?"

"I wouldn't go that far," I said, remembering the faceless "stranger" in my dream. "After all, kissing is an expression of emotion more than anything else, and the stronger the passion you're feeling—"

"—the better the kiss'll seem," Denny said, looking a bit crestfallen.

"But hey, by the same token, a great make-out session can boost a relationship to a whole new level," I quickly pointed out. "No matter what, Denny, the fact you cared enough to come in and ask about this at all can only mean good things for you and Kristen on prom night."

He brightened up again and said, "I hadn't thought of it that way."

⌒

"Marissa and I have gotten really tight over the past few months, and we're thinking that maybe on prom night we'll, you know, go the distance," Travis Meehan said. Travis was junior class vice president, a member of the varsity track team, and a fellow student in my French class. He was famously clean-cut, favoring striped button-down Oxford shirts and fleur-de-lis socks. I was surprised by his visit, and more than a little pleased, coming as it did after the now widely discussed resignation of star jock Eric Taschner from the PCN over the abstinence thing.

Travis and I had the usual talk about the risks and responsibilities that went with "going the distance," and he was so amazingly well versed on the subject that he could've written our sex pamphlet himself. "So what brings you here?" I finally asked.

"Even with all this stellar info, I still can't seem to make up my mind," he said. "I mean, I know my friends are all doing it, so I'm definitely trailing the pack. . . ."

Since I'd become a counselor, I'd discovered that an amazing number of my peers hung out with incredibly fearless "friends."

"Hold it," I said, making the T gesture for a time-out. "What your buds do with their bodies should have *zilch* effect on what you do with yours, 'cause if something goes wrong, only *you,* and probably your partner, will have to face the fallout."

Travis moved to the edge of his chair and looked as if he was poised to bail on me.

This was a dicey job because you had to shoot straight but without blowing away the customer.

"If I came on too strong, I'm sorry," I said with a reassuring smile. "But you wouldn't believe the number of students I've talked to in the last five months who've gotten into major jams because of this frantic, self-defeating, I'd-better-do-it-soon-or-I'll-be-the-last-virgin-on-the-planet attitude. It makes me crazy."

Travis nodded, eased back into his chair, and took some time to think.

After a while I said, "Your command of sex ed stats amazes. You thinking of going after Gerwin's job?"

"Not even!" Travis said, and we laughed. "No, my mom and dad are charter members of that new group Parents for Total Teen Abstinence. They give me lots of nutritious reading material, and I pretty much devour it."

"They must really care about you," I said.

"Yeah, I guess so. But sometimes I feel like

they're going to smother me with all of their love and concern, you know?"

I nodded.

"They'd totally freak, for instance, if they knew I was having this conversation with you."

"That's why it's confidential," I said. "But let's get back to your problem. If having sex would go against your values, then I'd definitely put it off. Based on what I've seen around here, I'd have to guess you'd just feel guilty and gross about yourself afterward."

"But it's not *my* values that are causing the problem here!" he said, giving me a deeply pained look. "*I* want to have sex with Marissa, and I think it's cool to 'cause I love her. A *lot*. I'm only in here right now because my folks have messed up my head so badly that I can't see straight, and I was sort of hoping you'd . . ." His voice trailed off.

"Hoping I'd what?"

He shrugged and gazed out the window.

Sometimes in this job you get mad at a counselee, and as the silence dragged on, I got plenty ticked at Travis. Sure, he was in a bad space, and I sympathized, but I was getting the distinct impression that he wanted me to make some kind of decision for him here, and I hated being put in that position.

Finally I said, "You've got a lot of baggage to sort through here, Travis. Maybe you'd like me to tell you that your mom and dad's values stink like yesterday's fish sticks, but that's not what I'm about here. Besides, we *all* carry our parents around in our heads, for better or worse, and you're not gonna get around that."

He still wasn't looking at me, but he seemed to be listening, so I chugged right on: "Why not just kick back on the sex thing for a while? Don't set the prom up as some kind of lame do-or-die deadline for 'losing' your virginity. . . . Maybe it would help you at this point to talk to a regular guidance counselor, someone who could give you professional insights—"

"No!" Travis said, pounding his fist on the desk. "No more adult advice!"

So he *was* listening.

"I'm sorry," he said, rubbing the desktop as if he'd injured it. "Look, Becca, even if I agree with you now that I'm not ready to make it with Marissa, what if I change my mind on prom night?"

"That's a killer-good question, Travis," I said, relieved to have him conversing again. "Fortunately, it takes two to tango. Have you talked over your worries with Marissa?"

He nodded. "And she's real understanding, too, up to a point. . . . I know this might sound crazy, but I think she wants to have sex at least as much as I do!"

"You thought guys had a total monopoly on these kinds of longings, did ya?" I asked with a smile.

Travis smiled back sheepishly.

"I know this might sound clichéd," I told him, "but it's as true for girls as it is for guys: if Marissa *really* loves you, she won't pressure you into making love before you're ready."

Travis nodded. "Oh yeah, she's aces. It's *me* I'm worried about."

"Let's sum up what we know about you, then. You're as well tuned to the risks involved as any counselee I've ever talked to. And you know there's a horbugulous pile of unsettled issues standing between you and a clear-headed decision. If, knowing all this, you still think you might end up wanting to go the distance on prom night, then I have one more reality check for you. Get thee to a drugstore and buy some condoms."

Travis blanched, looked away from me, and slowly shook his head. "Uh-uh. No way! I just can't see myself doing that."

I figured as much. "You've found your answer then, Travis," I told him. "You can't possibly be ready."

He thought that over and then nodded despondently.

⌒

I was feeling spent after Travis left—all the other peer counselors'd long since called it a day—and I was busy getting ready to lock up the trailer and head home when there was a loud knock on the door. I looked through the window at the tear-streaked face of Darla Swanson.

"I just broke up with Jeff," she said as I welcomed her inside.

"I'm sorry, Darla," I said, totally shocked that she'd actually come to see me.

"Don't be." She sniffled as she pulled a mirror out of her Saks Fifth Avenue handbag and studied her face. Even with tear tracks, it was a stunner: gorgeous, almond-shaped brown eyes; a straight, delicate nose; full lips; high cheekbones; and a fine, rounded chin. "I've already got a new guy," she said without much pride or joy. "He's captain of the tennis team at Primavera High School. We've been running into each other for years at league tournaments, and I started seeing him more seriously over the last few weeks." She wiped her tears away with her own tissue, snapped the hand mirror shut, and returned it to the bag.

"I know that sounds awful," she continued, "especially after what Peter Karona did to you, but you should hear me out first before you pass judgment."

"I'm not here to get judgmental," I assured her, struggling to stay ahead of this dizzying flood of info, "but you can't expect me to be an objective listener, especially considering my relationship with Jeff—"

"But that's exactly why I came here," she said. "I figured you of all people could see why I finally had to give up on him."

I gave in after about two seconds. "Okay. But I can only listen to you as a—"

"—friend," Darla said, graciously completing the sentence for me.

"Right. Not as a peer counselor."

She rolled her eyes. "You sound just like Jeff: 'I'm talking to you as an editor now, Darla. That feature about eating disorders on the cheerleading squad has potential, but you need to nail down at least two more interviews to make it credible.'"

It was a primo impression of Jeff at his most obnoxious.

"That's exactly the kind of thing that drove me nuts!" she went on. "The *Beacon* is just a high school newspaper, but he treats it as if it were the real thing."

"Maybe to him it is," I said.

"Right, which makes him an A-one editor in chief and a bargain-basement boyfriend. Jeff was always so damn busy and preoccupied. He had time for practically everybody's problems and needs except mine. Honest to God, the week before the *Beacon* went to press, I could've walked naked around his computer station playing love songs on an accordion and I seriously doubt he'd've noticed. Do you know he hadn't the slightest clue I'd started seeing another guy? You figure most people would pick up the signals and figure out that something's wrong, but not Jeff! All he cares about are his precious deadlines."

I thought about Peter suddenly and felt super uneasy. Had the Cindy thing happened because I was so preoccupied with the PCN? "But maybe Jeff figured he could trust you. And if you had all these issues workin' your nerves, Darla, why didn't you bring them out in the open?"

She gave me a guilty look and then an angry one. "That only works if a guy is willing to listen. I had give-and-take with Jeff up until about February, when his mom moved out. Now his parents are going through a divorce that makes my mom and dad's breakup look like a schoolyard scrape, and Jeff's reaction has been to just shut down emotionally, at least where *personal* feelings are concerned."

"I've seen that pattern before."

"You mean your little brother," Darla said sympathetically. "It's funny. I'll bet you're one of the few people around who could actually help Jeff talk through some of this stuff, but since he blames therapy for his parents' divorce—"

"What?!"

"Oh yeah—I forget you wouldn't know any of this. Jeff thinks his parents' marriage started its downhill slide after his mom started seeing a therapist last spring. She picked all kinds of fights with his dad, he says. But, of course, he also told me on other occasions that his parents'd been clawing at each other like wildcats ever since he was a little kid. The guy can be maddeningly inconsistent!"

"Yet you sound as if you still care about him," I pointed out, trying hard to maintain some objectivity.

Darla nodded. "I think I just got tired, Becca. I hung on for as long as I could because there's a lot of things about Jeff that are really awesome. He's smart, he's passionate, he makes things happen. And God, the way he kisses—I just can't describe it."

I was hoping she wouldn't try, either, but then her eyes started to gleam and I braced myself.

"I remember last Christmas at the Luna Point boat parade. My dad's yacht was sparkling, and JOY TO THE WORLD was spelled out in red-and-green lights on a giant net hanging down from the Ballard estate on the Luna Bluffs."

I closed my eyes and found myself at Casino Point again. The clock tower on the hillside was just beginning to strike twelve.

"I had on this tight-fitting red Santa's helper dress with white fuzzy trim. Jeff was decked out in this adorable red-and-green felt Santa's elf costume—I had to beg him to wear it, of course—and I pulled him into the master stateroom, where we yanked off our caps and kissed for what seemed like hours, until I completely melted in his arms and said, 'You're the best Christmas present I've ever had.'"

"But that feeling is gone now," I said hoarsely as I opened my eyes, shifted around in my chair, and tried once more to shake off that overpowering sense of longing.

" 'Fraid so," she said glumly. "The only things he seems to feel passionate about these days are the *Beacon* . . . and you."

"Me?"

"Sure. You know, the editorial give-and-take over the PCN, the fireworks show at the *Beacon* staff meeting two weeks ago, et cetera.

After that it got to the point where Jeff'd mention you on an almost daily basis—nearly always to slam you, of course, except when he was carrying on about what a great writer you are—but it still wore on me after a while."

"Hey, there's never been *anything* between us—," I began.

She laughed. "Don't you think I know that! You two were born on the straight and narrow." Then she said more seriously, "Blowing off a person you care about in favor of your work can be just as bad as cheating on them, though."

"Did you ever tell Jeff that?"

"Yes, lots of times! And he always promised to 'do better.' He could never actually bring himself to *apologize,* though. . . ."

"How well I remember that," I said, and we smiled at each other.

Darla checked her watch. "I'm keeping you way too late. Thanks loads for hearing me out . . . and maybe I can return the favor in a small way. That pest Eddie Ballard has drawn up a prom list, with me at the top. He actually saw fit, for some reason, to show it to me after I turned him down for the third consecutive time—this is all while I'm still going out with Jeff, mind you!—and I'm afraid I saw your name on it—"

"I know all about the list," I said quickly. "And I've already told him I'm not interested."

"That's good," Darla said, nodding, "because he thought of you as his 'safety date,' which means he's exhausted the list now, and we might all be spared his obnoxious presence at the prom."

"I was *number ten?!* I could throttle that little weasel!"

"You think being number *one* on his list was some kind of honor, do you?" Darla asked dryly, and then we both laughed.

As we walked to the parking lot together she said, while flipping her shiny, curly, high-maintenance, dark brown locks back over the shoulders of her white, short-sleeved pointelle cardigan, "Have you given any more thought to coloring your hair?"

My hair has a slight natural wave to it, which I've always been happy with, and I usually let it grow to about six inches beyond shoulder length. I was never too concerned, one way or another, about my quasimedium brown, blond-streaked hair color until last fall at a *Beacon* party held in Darla's palatial home. One of her many toys was a computer imaging machine that let you see how you'd look in a wide range of different hair colors and styles. We really had a blast with it, putting dreadlocks on Jeff, a red punker cut on Darla, an orange clown wig on Eddie, and so on. We tried traditional styles, too, and everybody seemed to be really taken by how I looked in an even medium brown shade, with golden summer highlights around my face. I never took the idea of recoloring my hair all that seriously, though. It hadn't done a thing for Roger.

"I have no plans to dye," I told her. "I guess I just don't feel 'passionate' enough about it."

She laughed and said, "I was only asking because I remembered how much Jeff liked your computer makeover."

Hey—what was she getting at here?

"Well," I said dismissively, "then maybe he can ask my computer image to the prom. They'd make a terrific couple. Both are rigid, two-dimensional, and totally uncommunicative."

Darla laughed, gave me five, and split off toward her car.

I stopped by a drugstore on the way home and took a casual, noncommittal tour of the hair-care section.

Chapter 11

T HE CALL CAME in at around 4:45 A.M. on Wednesday.

"They're firing!" rasped the voice on the phone.

"I think you have the wrong number," I said groggily.

"*No comprende,* dudettamente! We're talkin' double overhead out of the southwest here! Perfect, peeling tubes and not a kook in sight."

My surfer self suddenly roared to life, like a fuel-flooded camp stove when the match finally takes. This was Zoner on the line, and he was talking *monster waves!* "High on the hoot meter?" I asked as I sat up at attention.

"Off the scale, Becca my girl. One hundred and ten percent *pure stoke!*"

"Should I call Kayla?"

"Already done. Shall we wing by your dwelling in about fifteen?"

"Let there be surf!"

I splashed some water on my face, swished the sleep out of my mouth, brushed out my hair and pulled it back into a ponytail, yanked on a wet suit, downed some orange juice, left a note for Mom, grabbed my board out of the garage, and caught the Zoner express in just the nick of time.

Our conveyance was an old sunflower yellow rust-pocked 1961 Sahara Vista wagon. It featured whitewall tires and a Sphinx-shaped hood ornament and seemed to be held together in key spots by stickers for various types of surf products (CREATURES OF LEISURE BOARD COVERS), destinations (SURF COSTA RICA), and environmental causes (JOIN THE SURFRIDER FOUNDATION). The front bench seat was basically upholstered in silver duct tape, and the back of the vehicle was hollowed out to accommodate a max number of boards.

Kayla and Zoner looked so highly torqued you'd've thought they'd been awake and alert for hours. It wasn't just the prospect of epic surf that had them on edge, though; they were sitting as far apart from each other in the front seat as space would allow. Once I got situated between them, they both seemed to relax.

"In this dream last night, I had one of those near-death experiences," Zoner said as we sputtered down the nearly empty predawn streets of Luna Point. "But instead of seeing that comforting white light I'd been led to expect by all those TV specials, I beheld this mammoth bowl of Cocoa Pebbles and heard a voice thunder, 'PART OF YOUR COMPLETE BREAKFAST!' What do you girls think it means?"

Kayla and I burst out laughing.

"I also had this dream that I showed up at school wearing nothing but a pair of Velcro briefs," he went on in a perfect deadpan, "and the gnarly thing was, I really had to pee."

We laughed even harder this time and almost upset the plastic palm tree Zoner kept situated on the dashboard for good surf karma.

"What kind of peer counselors are you, anyway?" he asked, taking mock offense. "That second dream ended up causing me a lot of pain!"

He went on like this for a while, until we were so winded from laughter we had to beg him to stop.

When we got to the lot at the beach, though, our mouths clammed and our ears perked for that unmistakable pulsing thud. We got out of the car in our bare feet and felt the vibrations of the shorepound rippling through the asphalt. We ran up to the first rise in the sand and beheld the cool, blue-gray, mirror-smooth, six-to-eight-foot walls roaring shoreward under dawn's early light. Only a handful of surfers were out at this point, which would leave us plenty of room for thrills *and* spills with no fear of hassling drop-ins. "This is as core as it gets," Zoner said excitedly as we went back to fetch our sticks. "Be careful out there, girls, and don't hesitate to bail shoreward if you're getting hammered."

"We got it wired," Kayla said confidently. In spite of Zoner's objections that it was inappropriate for these conditions, she'd brought her new lighter board. I, on the other hand, had Moby with me.

Zoner paddled out first, caught one early, and went pedal-to-the-metal down a barreling groove, sliced up to the lip, pulled a floater down the falls, cut back up into the groove again, and finally threw his fist into the air and howled in triumph as he bailed out at the end.

Kayla would also manage several fine rides over the next hour or so—her aerials, especially, continued to amaze—but I, much to my chagrin, was eating it on virtually every wave I challenged. I dumped the takeoff on the first really good one and bailed in the trough on the second before I realized I was just too preoccupied to focus. So I paddled outside for a while and settled for floating over the humps.

My problem was yesterday'd been quite the raw experience. Eddie Ballard came by the trailer in the A.M. and took me to task for "being cruel and insensitive" to him on the phone Saturday night. "That's no way for a therapist to act," he said.

I wasted no time in straightening him out. "Don't think for even a second you can use my role as a peer counselor as a means to abuse me as a person, Eddie," I told him. "Now that you've exhausted that horrendously ill-conceived prom list of yours, I suggest you take some time out to examine why a person with all your resources and potential has managed to alienate so many people at this high school."

When he then became verbally abusive and vowed to take some sort of vague 'revenge' on me, I angrily insisted that he leave (while keeping my hands entirely to myself). He broke at that point and got all morose and apologetic before finally sulking out the door.

Later Elaine Stillwell came in to see me. "I met with Walt, like you suggested, and it went really well at first. I think having sex so soon really *did* freak him out, and he was totally relieved that I didn't hold it against him. We agreed to 'downshift,' as he put it. We went to a movie with friends last Friday night, and all we did was hold hands—it was totally great! We remade our prom plans, too. But then last night, we were doing math homework at his house and there was no one else home . . . and he tried to talk me into having sex with him again. When I started to explain why that'd be a bad idea, he got all hyper and basically threw me out!"

I felt bad for Elaine, who was crying by this point, but not nearly so awful as I would've felt if she'd given *in* to his pressure. She was way bummed about the prom again, of course, but I told her that if she still wanted to go, she was welcome to hang with me.

"What if you get a date?" she wondered.

"That's not gonna happen," I said with a laugh. "And even if it does, my invitation to you still stands." That seemed to cheer her up a lot.

Now, as *el sol* slowly rose up into the sky behind Saddleback Mountain and the Luna Bluffs turned the color of gold foil, I got the uneasy feeling that the humps beneath me were getting larger. Time to catch a relatively small but juicy one, I decided, and ride it into the beach.

I successfully paddled my way onto one of the few remaining user-friendly six-footers, crouched into a trim stretch, and began what looked to be my one and only decent ride of the morning. I brushed my fingers on the glassy face and watched the lip glisten and sparkle with transparent splendor in the early morning sunlight.

And then for no good reason at all, my mind arced back to yesterday again. Jeff Gardiner had confronted me as I left my lunch table. His breakup with Darla was by then public knowledge, and I felt bad for him, but the question he directed at me and the tone he used were still way out of line:

"Did Darla come to you for counseling yesterday afternoon?" he demanded.

"That's confidential info, Jeff. You of all people should know that—"

"Did she talk to you about my parents?" he persisted. I thought I saw some real anxiety in his eyes now. The great and powerful Wizard of Oz was obviously terrified that Dorothy'd gotten a peek behind the curtain and discovered he was just as frail and human as the rest of us. "I can't have this conversation with you, Jeff. I'm sorry," I said coolly as I turned away from him and started off toward class.

"And people call *me* a power-tripper!" he shouted at my back.

I spent the rest of the day and most of the

evening worrying about whether or not I had in fact abused my position by talking to Darla. But the bottom line was she'd sought *me* out, not vice versa. And we'd talked *expressly* as friends.

The wave I'd carelessly lost track of suddenly picked me up and dipped me, fondue-style, into the shallows. Conditions were a lot more turbulent than last Saturday, and for about ten seconds I twirled like an Olympic figure skater in the award round. I angrily clawed my way back up to the light, cursing myself for wasting such a beautiful wave on Jeff Gardiner. When I broke the surface, I took in a few huge gulps of air, reeled in Moby, and with a feeling of defeat, headed for the high ground. When I got there, I was startled to see two surfers contemplating their broken boards. One of them was Zoner!

"Where's Kayla?!" I asked him anxiously.

He shook his head, pointed out at the lineup, and said in a very worried voice, "I told her she'd better come in, that conditions were getting way too intense, but she just blew me off. The growler I rode in on chewed me up and spit me out, as you can plainly see."

He gestured at his ruined board. "I don't know what *she's* thinking. . . ."

But I did.

I ran down to the shoreline. Kayla was relatively easy to spot because there were now more surfers on the beach than there were in the water. This, in and of itself, was a major danger sign. "KAYLA!" I screamed over the roar of the surf. "COME IN NOW!"

Kayla heard me and held up her index finger, apparently to indicate "just one more."

Zoner arrived at my side, holding one-half of his board up above his head as the ultimate warning sign. Kayla didn't see it, though, because she was already in the process of lining herself up for the next wave, a fat, hissing monster that was *easily* double-overhead for her. "She's gonna get creamed," Zoner said unhappily as he tossed the useless chunk of fiberglass aside.

Kayla actually made such a clean, controlled launch, though, that it looked to me like she might pull it off after all.

But gradually I came to realize what Zoner obviously knew already: Kayla just flat out lacked the strength and skill needed to tackle a barrel of this magnitude. It finally buried her with the cruel, cold inevitability of a mountain avalanche. I screamed once as she disappeared under the thundering white wall of Pacific spume and then again moments later as her board rocketed skyward and the leash broke.

"It's a blitz!" Zoner cried out (this was a call to arms meaning "Surfer in trouble!"), and there was an impressive rush of bodies toward the section of froth where Kayla'd gone down. Precious seconds ticked by with no sign of her, as a battalion of equally powerful waves continued their inevitable assault on the beach. We rushed around frantically, sloshing our arms through the water in search of a solid floating object.

It was Zoner who spotted her hand flailing around in the foam, and he shouted out triumphantly, "I found her!" He hauled her limp form out of the water and carried her as fast as he could to the beach, nearly falling over at one point under the impact of yet another wave.

Zoner laid her out in dry sand and immediately cupped his ear over her mouth to listen for breathing. He nodded. We found no sign of broken bones. "Kayla," he said gently as he

held and patted one hand and I did the same with the other. "Wake up, girl."

She opened her lagoon-blue eyes slowly, looked directly at Zoner, and suddenly burst out crying. She sluggishly rolled away from him toward me and said miserably, "Don't let 'im see me like this, Becky." Then she began to cough up seawater.

"Why'd she say that? What goes on?!" Zoner asked me.

I figured things couldn't possibly sink any lower than this, so I said, "She's in love with you, Zoner, okay? She wants to go to the prom with you." Kayla squeezed my hand tightly as I told him.

"Well, sure, I love her, too," he said, as if this were the most obvious thing in the world. Several of the surfers gathered around us began to murmur to each other; your typical major wipeout wasn't usually followed by declarations of this sort.

Kayla let go of my hand and rolled back over to face the Zoneman. "What are"—*huah*—"you talking a"—*cough*—"bout?" she wheezed.

"I've been hot on you for ages, babe," he said, "but I was afraid if I bared these feelings

and you found them hurlworthy, our budship would be pushin' up ice plant. And then Becca here told me you were in love with some guy—"

"That would be you," I said with a fast-growing sense of irony.

"What about"—*cough, cough*—"Sabrina's" —*huuuaaahhh*—"cousin Brandi?" Kayla asked him.

"She's for real but not in my plans. I had Barney hip you to her existence and intentions only so you'd know I'd become prom-willing."

Which would explain why Barney'd winked at me on Saturday.

"You know, I'll bet a peer counselor would've advised us to handle this whole thing in a much more straightforward manner," I said, and the two of us who could breathe had a good, long laugh.

"Becca, please help me up now," Kayla asked me a few minutes later. I did so and getting vertical prompted another coughing fit. After it passed, she gestured for Zoner to come closer.

"Kiss me, you surf bum, before I"—*cough, cough*—"fully regain my consciousness and

change my mind about you," she whispered with a big ol' grin. And so he did, with considerable gusto, to the hoots and high fives of a greatly enthused assembly.

Shortly thereafter, a surfer came running up from the shoreline with the two halves of Kayla's board in hand. He gave them to me, and I placed them directly beside Zoner's. I then gestured at the four fiberglass-'n'-foam fragments and said to their embracing owners, "Can I ask you guys a prom-related question?"

They nodded.

"Do you dance any better than you surf?"

For some reason, they started throwing sand at me.

Chapter 12

ZONER AND KAYLA dropped me off at home and said they'd probably come into school a period or two late, depending on how fast Kayla rebounded. I rushed into the garage, propped up Moby, and then charged into the apartment to shower, consume, and head for school. There was no possible way I'd make it to the trailer by seven, but Vickie Coolidge was scheduled to counsel that morning and she had a key of her own, so I figured, no problem.

Wrong!

Mom'd already left for work, but she'd written me a note saying there were several messages waiting for me on the answering machine:

"Becca, this is Jeff, calling from the *Beacon*. You're probably on your way to school by now, but I thought you should know that there's something really weird going down in front of your trailer. I'm walking over to investigate. . . ." *Beep.*

"Hey, Becca, this is Vickie. For all I know you're getting to campus right this second, but I decided to call you at home anyway, just in case you were running late. A district police officer is putting special security locks on our trailer doorknobs! I asked him why, and he was super vague about the reason. He thinks one of our counselors violated a district code or something. He slapped this big orange sign on the side of the trailer that says: CLOSED UNTIL FURTHER NOTICE BY ORDER OF THE BOARD OF EDUCATION, LUNA POINT UNIFIED SCHOOL DISTRICT. It's all too Orwellian for me. . . ." *Beep.*

"*'Violated a district code'?!*" My heart was racing now and I was filled with a gargantuan sense of dread as I moved on to the last message:

"Hi, Becca, this is Mr. Gordon. . . . Doctor

Cayuso [the principal] just called me to say that Bernard Crampton has chosen the PCN for his latest political stunt. Crampton claims you instructed a seventeen-year-old boy to go out and buy a condom so that he could 'indulge in sex on prom night.' [Travis!] I'm sure that's not true, but I'm calling you now because I have a feeling you'll be required to make a full accounting of your actions at tonight's emergency school board meeting, which Crampton is in the process of arranging even as I speak. Come by to see me in my office ASAP, and we'll talk strategy. . . ." *Beep.*

My head was whirling. They'd actually put locks on the trailer, as if we'd been selling drugs in there or something! It didn't seem possible!

I anxiously retrieved my counseling journal and ran through the notes I'd taken at the session with Travis and then reviewed them over and over in my head as I showered, dressed, and downed a tall glass of milk. I was sure I'd stayed within the legal bounds. But would that even *matter?*

(And why on earth had Jeff Gardiner cared enough to call me?)

When I got to campus at about 7:20, Dr.

Cayuso was already ordering the district police officer to remove the padlocks from the trailer, and the officer was raising a stink about authorization. "Someone has already alerted the news media to this unfortunate turn of events, Officer Roberts, and the phones are ringing off the hook in my main office," Dr. Cayuso told him. "Now do you think I want my school to look like some sort of prison camp when it appears on the six o'clock news?" Our principal had piercing dark brown eyes; an attractive, no-nonsense face; and, when she chose to employ it, a formidable scowl.

Officer Roberts looked at her uncertainly for a moment, then said, "Why no, ma'am, I don't think you'd want that at all" as he promptly got to work on removing the locks.

Dr. Cayuso greeted me with a warm, friendly smile and a firm handshake. "The locks are coming off, Becca," she said, taking me aside from the large group of curious students and bewildered counselors who'd gathered to check out the action. "But I don't have the authority to actually let you in there until this is all straightened out. You know I support the PCN—you've helped a lot of kids when they needed it most—but this," she said, gesturing at Officer Roberts, "is unfortunately about a lot more than peer counseling."

"I understand, Dr. Cayuso," I said. "But how can Mr. Crampton resort to these kinds of strong-arm tactics, especially after he got so badly burned on the freedom of expression thing last year?!"

"He's an elected official," she said in a carefully measured tone. "Mr. Crampton will do whatever he sees fit to serve the vital interests of his particular constituency. . . . I'm sure you've learned by now that democracy is not always a savory business." Two boys having a scuffle over by the industrial arts building suddenly knocked over a trash can. "And neither is being a principal," Dr. Cayuso added resignedly as she went over to intervene.

I eased back into the crowd to calm my fellow counselors and hipped them to the fact that the trailer was still off-limits to us, at least for today. "I'm going to see Mr. Gordon right now, though, and he seems pretty optimistic that we'll pull through this okay. In the meantime, go ahead and take advantage of this lockout by meeting with your counselees in less cramped quarters. Like maybe a phone booth." A few counselors laughed, but most of them still looked majorly stressed, and I found myself wishing that Kayla and Zoner were here to help me cope. I apologized to the handful of counselees who'd come to see me specifically, made other arrangements with them, and then took off toward the guidance counseling office.

As I passed under the large stucco-and-adobe arch that had LUNA POINT HIGH SCHOOL—HOME OF THE SEA HAWKS emblazoned on it in the school colors of red and white, I nearly collided with Jeff Gardiner. He said he'd been looking for me.

"I assume you know the full scoop now?" he asked with obvious excitement.

"Yeah, unfortunately, I do." I told him briefly about who I'd heard from and talked to, so far, and thanked him for his message.

"I've made anonymous calls to a bunch of local and regional media outlets for you," he said. "There seems to be a lot of interest in this story. And why not? It's a real grabber. You've got the prom, sex, teen therapy, sex, freedom-of-speech issues, sex. . . ."

I laughed, though I felt a bit let down. While I was glad to be rid of the creepy Jeff Gardiner who'd accosted me after lunch yesterday, I still had the distinct impression that he was only taking an interest in my crisis because it would make good copy. So I decided to call him on it. "Don't think I'm not grateful here, Jeff, but what gives? *They've shut down the PCN.* Isn't that exactly what you've been hoping for the last five months?"

Jeff shook his head and gazed down at his Nikes. "Not like this," he said. "If the PCN failed, I wanted it to be for lack of *student* support." He looked back up at me, his blue eyes focused and intense now. "But that sure hasn't happened, has it, Becca? To be honest, the mail from my last column is currently running three to one in your favor."

"Really?!" I said excitedly. "How many letters have there been so far?"

"Four," he said with a smirk, and we both laughed.

"So are you actually admitting that you were wrong about the PCN?" I asked hopefully. There was a stray lock of platinum blond hair hanging down the middle of his forehead. It was really cute.

"Get real," he said, rolling his eyes. "This issue goes a lot deeper for me than you think."

I nodded with understanding and almost offered my sympathy over his parents' divorce. I caught myself just in the nick of time. "So . . . are you going to help me fight off Crampton?"

Jeff grinned. "We'll go straight for his Achilles' heel, which is still the free-speech issue."

I grinned back and told him I'd been thinking along those same lines already.

"I'll get an all-day pass from Ms. Sullivan, you get one from Mr. Gordon, and we'll meet in the library second period to start brainstorming," he said.

"Just like the old days." I hugged the notebook I was carrying super tightly and my toes scrunched up in my shoes.

"If you say so," Jeff replied casually.

～

When I got to Mr. Gordon's office I was surprised—and more than a little relieved—to find that he was already talking to Travis Meehan. Travis told us what happened. "I had a long talk with Marissa on Monday night, and then I decided to try that 'reality check' you suggested. I went out yesterday after school and actually bought a box of condoms. You should've seen me; my hands were shaking the whole time at the register. But I did it. And I *still* wasn't sure if I was ready for sex. Anyway, I brought 'em home and then sped back to school for a nighttime class council meeting. I guess my mom must've noticed something weird in how I was acting because she searched my bedroom right after I left and found the condoms.

"I won't go into the gruesome details, but suffice to say I came home to a wicked awful scene. Marissa's never allowed to step foot in my parents' house again, and I've been forbidden to attend the prom.... (Travis faltered here.) Anyway, my parents wanted to know all about how I got the idea to buy the condoms in the first place. As if the things aren't advertised all over the place, right? I was pretty played out by that point, and I did what turned out to be a stupid thing. I told them about our counseling session.

He shook his head. "Instead of helping them to see how sane and sensible buying condoms was, like I'd hoped, I just ended up giving them someone else to blame. My folks called their school board buddy Mr. Crampton, and now, as you know, he's planning to shut your whole network down.... (Travis faltered again.) You've got to believe I didn't mean for this to happen, Becca! I'm so sorry!"

I gave him a long, reassuring hug and told him not to sweat it. Then we ran through his counseling session together and found that we'd interpreted it in basically the same way.

"I don't think Crampton really expected to use Travis as some kind of witness against the PCN," Mr. Gordon said as he hooked his thumbs through his rainbow-colored suspenders and tugged at them thoughtfully. "I talked to Cathy Irwin, the school board president, about a half hour ago. She's a real fan of the PCN—probably without knowing it, you helped her best friend's daughter through a very tough Christmas last year. Anyway, Irwin says Crampton is really just maneuvering to force a board referendum on the hot-button topic of sex ed before the June elections. Here's how the political math breaks down: Cathy Irwin and Jason Woods are firmly behind us, while Ofelia Roberts and Crampton are both PTTA members. Which leaves Winslow Taggert as the swing vote."

"And Mr. Taggert is up for reelection," Travis said.

"Which means we're toast," I said forlornly.

Mr. Gordon shook his head. "Taggert's nobody's toady. But if you're going to sell him on peer counseling, Becca, you'll have to be good and sharp and avoid getting sidetracked into a debate about things like 'condom distribution on high school campuses and its contribution to the decline of all things American.' "

I laughed, but Travis said in a serious voice, "It'll be impossible to avoid that line of argument completely."

"I know that only too well," Mr. Gordon said ruefully. "I've suffered through several recent board meetings."

"I think we should focus on the issue of free speech," I said. "Jeff Gardiner has already offered to help me out with that angle, and if you can give me a day pass, I'll get to work on it with him starting next period."

Mr. Gordon smiled. "I think that approach could really work with Taggert. . . . But how exactly did you manage to enlist the aid of our greatest student critic?"

I guess I blushed, because Mr. Gordon started to laugh. "Never mind," he said. "Here's what I think you can expect to-night: Crampton and Robbins will come at you like gangbusters, and you're gonna have to stand firm all on your own. Much as we'd like to, Doctor Cayuso and I can't really go to bat for you in this situation. The board wants to hear from a living, breathing teen peer counselor and not a well-intentioned fac-ulty member or administrator acting as a proxy. You've been put on the spot, Becca, and you've gotta show the board just how wrong the PTTA is about your intents and purposes."

My stomach felt sort of queasy now, and I was starting to actually feel nostalgic about that morning's monster surf.

"If you want to run role plays, I can fill the part of Crampton for you," Travis offered. "I know all his arguments."

"That'd be great!" I told him.

"I figure it's the least I can do," he said with a deep sigh.

Jeff, Travis, and I—and by fourth period, Zoner and Kayla—worked almost nonstop on fact-gathering, argument-structuring, and simulated verbal warfare. As word got out that we'd hunkered down in the library, Elaine Stillwell and several other counselees came by and offered to speak before the board on our behalf. Kayla, Zoner, and I thanked them all and eagerly encouraged them to show up that night, but we also made it clear we didn't want anyone to compromise themselves by describing, in a public forum, the very personal problems and issues that'd brought so many of them to the PCN in the first place. Besides, we'd already heard through Mr. Gordon that so many parents were phoning the board office to demand the right to speak at tonight's meeting, it was doubtful there'd even be time for student testimonials.

At lunch the four of us (Travis, for obvious reasons, was keeping a low profile) were interviewed under the photogenic main arch by the local press and TV media, and we thought the whole thing went pretty well. I defended the need for teen peer counseling and tried to lighten up the proceedings a bit by concluding with the observation: "We teenagers don't pretend to fully understand you adults. You seem kind of standoffish at times and prone to severe mood swings. Your popular tastes are worlds apart from our own and your value judgments occasionally strike us as both arbitrary and ill-considered. But we want you to know that we love you anyway and trust that, over the long haul, you'll give us reason to be proud."

Jeff did the Patrick Henry thing: "You can't teach us about the proud American tradition of free discourse for eleven-plus years and then expect us to sit idly by when it is taken away arbitrarily, without any pretense of due process!"

Kayla posed this puzzler: "If God meant for teenagers to totally ignore the subject of sex"—*cough*—"then why'd he see fit to juice us up with all these extra hormones?"

And finally Zoner warned ominously that if the discussion of condoms was banned on campus, "talk of dancing would almost certainly go next."

Chapter 13

THE SIX HUNDRED-SEAT auditorium at Luna High was packed. The five board members sat behind a table on stage, under a big array of superbright lights. I'd felt primed for this challenge earlier in the evening when I put on my mom's green power suit, but now, looking up at this awesome jury of powerful adults, I felt like a poser, a mere tyke playing at dress-up.

Thousands of words and legions of agitated parents preceded my turn at the podium, and at times it seemed like the whole scene might just erupt and go totally out of control. When a motion was passed to link the fate of the prom pamphlet with that of the PCN, the pressure on yours truly became all-time.

As I made my way up to the podium, I got that panicky get-me-the-hell-out-of-here-before-I-croak feeling that'd dogged me as a novice surfer. But I couldn't bail now. Way too many people were counting on me! I launched my presentation with the customary greetings and was so freaked at first by the sound of my own amplified voice that, like a total dork, I actually looked around the auditorium to see who else was speaking.

But then I chilled by remembering that Kayla, Zoner, Jeff, Mr. Gordon, the PCN staff, and five months' worth of counselees were all literally right behind me, sending positive vibes my way. This gave me the confidence I needed to charge: "Not one of the many parents who've spoken up for the PCN tonight—and we're super grateful to all of you—has said that they're in favor of teens having sex on prom night. (pause) I'm not here to take that line, either. Truth be told, I've been called up tonight for one reason only: to defend the fact that I subscribe to the notion—which some in this auditorium have openly declared to be a bogus one—that we teens share in common with you adults certain basic, inalienable rights, among them the right to freedom of expression."

There was loud applause from the students in the audience, and Ms. Irwin quickly gaveled them into silence. She was wearing an impressive dark red suit with shiny gold buttons. I wondered if she was ticked at me for getting a rise out of the crowd, but since her emotions were currently hidden behind a world-class poker face, there was no way for me to tell.

I went on to talk about constitutional law as it related to teens (this was Jeff's contribution). Since in his earlier remarks Mr. Crampton had already invoked the U.S. Supreme Court's 1988 *Hazelwood* ruling to justify censoring (i.e., shutting down) the PCN, I cited the high court's 1969 *Tinker v. Des Moines* decision, which had established that students do not "shed their constitutional rights to freedom of speech or expression at the schoolhouse gate." Mention of this landmark ruling, which was not explicitly overturned by *Hazelwood,* set off a buzz in the audience.

I talked about how the PCN got started, ran through its brief history, and read excerpts from my recent flyer. I thanked Mr. Crampton for his long, emotional speech on the dangers of STDs, the fallibility of condoms and various other forms of birth control, and the epidemic of unwanted teen pregnancies. (Listening to Crampton I'd gotten the distinct impression that he genuinely *cared* about teens at risk; this clearly wasn't just political posing on his part, as I had assumed. Still, he was no champion of free speech, and that really rankled.)

Finally, feeling weak in the knees and hoarse in the throat, I cut to the chase: "We at the PCN have always emphasized, and will continue to stress, the indisputable fact that abstinence is the only one hundred percent safe-sex option. . . . But the use of police state tactics in a totally misguided attempt to make this the *only* option that can be freely discussed at Luna High—*that* we object to in the strongest possible terms!"

There was an uproar from the crowd, a lively mix of cheers, jeers, applause, and cries of protest. Ms. Irwin gaveled the audience into silence again, while Mr. Crampton whispered something into Ms. Robbins's ear. Mr. Taggert seemed to be taking copious notes and occasionally chewed thoughtfully on the tip of his pen. Mr. Woods favored me with a wink and a smile, which lowered my jackhammering heart rate just a bit.

The first question came from Ms. Robbins: "I realize this is an unusual query, Rebecca, but I think it's important that the board know something of your personal background so we can put your eloquent presentation into a proper perspective. Are you, yourself, sexually active?"

And some counselees thought *I* played hardball! Fortunately, I'd gotten hit with this question once in practice, so I wasn't totally unprepared for it. "N-no, Ms. Robbins," I stammered, "I-I myself am not . . . if you wanna know the truth, I don't even have a date to the prom."

That last part was a total ad-lib, but the crowd roared with laughter.

"She means," Mr. Crampton said in his deep bass voice as he struggled to be heard over the raucous yukfest, "are you still a *virgin?*"

His angry brown eyes seemed to drill right into me, and I was temporarily paralyzed into speechlessness.

"That's an outrageous question, Bernard!" Ms. Irwin snapped. "She doesn't have to answer that!"

Ms. Irwin's anger rallied my spirits. I leaned into the mike and said unsteadily, "With, um, all due respect, sir, my, uh, sexual history is . . . (I had to scramble for just the right words, and it took a few painful seconds) is no more a matter for public scrutiny than your own." *So there, you bully!*

The crowd went totally hyper, Crampton gave me the stink eye, Mr. Wood and Ms. Irwin laughed and applauded, and Mr. Taggert looked up from his notes and gazed at me directly for the first time. Somehow, miraculously, I seemed to actually be stumbling through this ordeal.

"Do you not agree, Rebecca, as well informed as you are," Ms. Robbins said in a distinctly less friendly tone than before, "that the only rational way for teens to protect themselves against sexually transmitted diseases is to practice abstinence?"

"That's a values question, ma'am, and I'm only really here to tackle the issue of free speech," I replied simply.

(Earlier that day Jeff'd advised me: "If they

throw a curveball at you, Becca, just swing at it with the First Amendment. That way you can't miss.")

"The two cannot be separated in this case," Mr. Crampton insisted.

I thought he was flat-out mad-dogging me now; it was really starting to piss me off. (And oddly enough, getting steamed seemed to calm my nerves a bit more.) "I beg to differ, sir. According to the best current stats available on this issue, well over two-thirds of unmarried women and men will have had sexual intercourse by the time they reach the age of twenty. That's why I feel you've asked a 'values' question." (Kayla got credit for chasing down these stats.)

"Shall we follow the herd, then, as it stampedes off a cliff?" Mr. Crampton asked.

God, this guy was relentless! He had a point about peer pressure, of course, and Zoner'd used this same herd metaphor in his slammin' prom definition, but I thought in this case the idea was being taken (literally) too far. "Shall we compare teenagers to cattle, so that we can lead them around by the nose?" I responded.

The teens in the audience cheered and the whole crowd got riled again, but I quickly plowed on: "Strained metaphors and stunning stats aside, I think we've all seen, in the parent speeches made here tonight, ample evidence that a superwide range of values exists here in Luna Point itself. A peer counselor, to be of any use at all, *has* to be wise to this fact."

"To the point that you would knowingly put your fellow students at risk for contracting potentially deadly diseases?" Ms. Robbins asked with alarm.

"You've got us peer counselors pegged all wrong," I protested. "We try to help our counselees make informed choices, *but there's no way we'd ever actually make those choices for them.*"

The grilling continued like this for almost another half-hour, until at last Ms. Irwin signaled that there was time for just one more question.

I was super relieved to hear that, 'cause by then I was pretty much played out.

The final query was a two-parter, and it came from Mr. Taggert: "Do you know, Ms. Singleton, approximately how many condoms are sold in the United States every year?"

I rummaged through my weary brain in search of the stat. Everything was coming more slowly now. "Over half a billion, sir," I finally said. (Zoner'd found that one.)

"Thank you," Mr. Taggert responded. Then he leaned back in his chair, folded his arms across his chest, and said to me, "Earlier this evening, my fellow board members Ms. Robbins and Mr. Crampton savaged the federal Centers for Disease Control and Prevention for their promotion of condom use. But they also freely cited the alarming statistics on STDs produced by that very same agency. Now I don't know whether I should trust the federal government or not! (The audience laughed.) Can you provide me, Rebecca, with an alternative, but equally authoritative voice, on this extremely vexing issue?"

Mr. Taggert was *helping* me, I realized with a growing sense of relief and excitement. My brain kicked back into high gear, and I quickly realized that, at around four-thirty that afternoon, I'd found just the thing he was now asking for: "The World Health Organization identifies condom use, along with education about sexual transmission of disease, to be the cornerstone of effective AIDS prevention programs around the globe, sir," I reported.

" 'Around the globe,' " Mr. Taggert repeated as he smiled broadly, put down his pen, and leaned forward to address the audience. "I can't speak for my fellow board members, but I for one feel fortunate to live in a land where a capable young woman like Ms. Singleton is free to marshall such an impressive array of information in the service of informed debate—"

Made bold by a growing sense that victory was at hand, I interrupted him at that point to draw attention to my "research staff" (except, of course, for Travis, who I'd have to thank later in private). The audience applauded the grinning trio, and Jeff looked surprisingly touched by my gesture.

"We're proud of you all," Mr. Taggert said. "And let me assure this assembly that I plan to cast my vote most enthusiastically in favor of continuing the Peer Counseling Network, with full confidence that it will continue to dispense its advice to our teenagers with the kind of thoroughness and even-handedness we've witnessed here tonight."

The audience went totally nuts, and I let loose with a megamongo sigh of relief. *The PCN was saved!*

Chapter 14

WHEN ALL THE heady post-board meeting interviews, handshakes, and hugs were
finally history, Kayla, Zoner, Jeff, and I motored to a minimart to snag some Dove Bars
before returning to my place (where we'd all
rendezvoused shortly before going to the
meeting in Jeff's car). Kayla and Zoner went
inside to make the purchase, while Jeff and I
stayed in the dimly lit front seat and talked
through the events of the day.

"You were really awesome up there," he
said for about the fifth time since we'd left the
auditorium. "You seemed so sure of yourself."

"It was a total illusion, but thanks. And you

know I couldn't've done it without you," I once again reminded him. It was the absolute truth, too. Jeff'd worked with me on every angle of the presentation; in fact, he hadn't really left my side since second period that morning!

And so I wondered: were his *true* feelings for me coming out now because Darla was gone from the picture, or was he just caught up in the temporary thrill of a battle well fought? And now that his hand was resting on the car seat only about an inch away from mine, should I take a chance on gauging his affection for me by reaching over and boldly taking hold of it, or would that be too much too soon? (Jeff's pupils were dilated, yes, but it was, after all, dark out. And he hadn't swallowed hard yet, at least not when I was watching.) Finally I scooted my hand about a quarter-inch closer to his, figuring if he then moved his hand, it would almost certainly mean—

"Got the treats, kiddies!" Zoner said as he opened the back door and got into the car.

Damn.

"I think he bought four bars just for him-

held it up out of my reach. "I only want to look up what I wrote to you last year," he said with a wry, suggestive smile.

He actually remembered! It'd meant something special to him, too! I wanted to die.

"You won't find it in there," Roger said mildly as he appeared suddenly in my doorway.

On second thought, maybe I wanted to *kill*.

Kayla soon appeared right behind Roger and gave me an anxious look that said, "I knew he was up to no good, but I couldn't stop him." And then Zoner showed behind Kayla. Where there's a serious accident, there's always a traffic jam. . . .

"What's your brother talking about?" Jeff asked with concern as he brought the annual down to eye level and flipped straight to page 47. There he saw the ragged blank square where his picture used to be, and the sparkle in his eyes died out.

Now I suppose this much *might've* happened even if Roger hadn't appeared in the doorway when he did; I'd've tried to explain the missing picture to Jeff with some sort of involuted but hopefully plausible story (a white lie—the deluxe version). But since

self," Kayla said with good-natured disgust as she also got in.

Jeff looked at my hand and then at me and smiled knowingly before reaching for the ignition and starting the car. So we *had* been on the same wavelength! Totally encouraged, I started sending major prom vibes his way and began to agonize over who should ask whom.

Zoner was already plotting out quite the unconventional preprom festivities, including a chauffeured hearse, a fast-food dining experience, and a predance trek to a bowling alley. (He and Kayla were totally cool about including Elaine Stillwell in the fun, too, once I explained how she was a stranded counselee and a kindred spirit.)

When we got to my place, Mom raved about having watched an excerpt of the board meeting on the tube and totally hosed us with praise before heading off to bed (she had an early A.M. meeting with a group of nuclear engineers). Roger made a point of congratulating each of us, with awkward formality, on a "job well done." (The swelling in his lip was gone and the scrape on his forehead had scabbed over; Mom'd readily accepted his "bike accident" story and, as predicted, didn't once inquire about the missing jacket.) Zoner offered Roger a Dove Bar, and he not only accepted it but actually sat down to hang with us for a few. He didn't say much, though, and mainly just stared at Jeff and me with this really bizarro smile. Truth be told, I was pretty much relieved when he finally bailed back to his room.

"Why don't you give Jeff a tour of your humble abode?" Kayla suggested. She'd been glowing nonstop since this morning, a phenomenon that'd led me to conclude that it was actually requited love and *not* the vitamin B-15 in garbanzo beans that improves your skin tone.

"I don't think Jeff is really interested—," I began.

"How 'bout we just cut to the chase and you show me your bedroom," Jeff said playfully as he licked the last remaining bit of ice cream off the stick. "That's where these tours always end up anyway."

"Oh my, we've got a man of the world here," I said with a laugh as I secretly thrilled at his suggestion.

"Well, awright, but don't stay up there

any too long," Zoner said in a naggin[g] as he shook his (third consecutive) D[o] at us. "I wasn't born yesterday. I kn[ow] youngsters've got only one thing o[n] mind!"

"Yeah," I said as we got up, "un[like] homework."

As it turned out, Jeff laid not a f[inger on] me and instead explored my room wi[th the] thoroughness of an investigative [reporter] prepping a major bio piece. He aske[d me] probing questions as he examined t[he] able holstein cow's head hanging [on my] door; the quilted bedspread that de[picts the] San Francisco waterfront in breath[taking de]tail; the posters of the L.A. Phil[harmonic,] Tom Hanks, Daniel Day-Lewis, a[nd] on Catalina Island; and my awards [. He] rummaged through my bookcases [and] eventually came across last year's [annual. He] smiled in a nostalgic way, pulled [it out,] began to flip through it. . . .

Oh my God!

"You don't want to waste yo[ur time with] that!" I said with way too much u[rgency as I] rushed over to relieve him of the [annual.]

Jeff thought I was just playing,

Roger *was* there now, I figured the only way to salvage this situation was to plead guilty right up front and hope that Jeff was better at accepting apologies than he was at offering them.

"Jeff," I began contritely, "I did a really lame and pathetic thing last week. Your last column got me really steamed, and . . ." I gave all the petty details and then sheepishly handed him the trash can. "Needless to say," I concluded as he stared dumbly into the receptacle, "I don't feel that way about you at all now, and I hope you'll accept my deepest apology." I took a split second to glare at Roger; he had the dazed and confused look of a hunter who'd just watched his quarry commit suicide.

Jeff suddenly started to laugh, and he put the can down. I yukked right along with him at first, totally stoked that he was taking this in such good spirits, but then I saw his face and realized he wasn't laughing *that* way at all.

"Too pathetic for words," he said, gesturing at the can. "Imagine what the people you won over tonight would think now, if they could only see this."

"They'd think: 'I've done stupid things like

that when I've been mad, too,' " I said as my heart sank.

"Oh, really?" Jeff said disgustedly. "Well shucks, I forgot for a sec that you can always see *exactly* what's going on in other people's heads."

"And just what is that supposed to mean?" I said, gearing up for battle. "I never made any such claim!"

"*Please* don't do this, you guys," Kayla said anxiously.

"Didn't you gain any insight into what I'm about tonight, Jeff?" I went on. "Or has it now become impossible to penetrate that thick wall of insecurity you call 'self-reliance'?"

"You counseling types live in constant fear of not being needed, don't you?" Jeff asked contemptuously.

"You're veering toward the boil here, kids," Zoner warned.

"*All* human beings are terrified by the thought of not being needed, Jeff! My God, you've lost Darla, your parents are divorcing, and yet you still strut around pretending like you're some kind of superman—"

"So you *did* talk to Darla! I should've known! Did you encourage her to blame me

for everything that went wrong in our relationship? Did you drool as she gave a thirdhand account of my family misfortunes? You
gossip-mongering phony! And to think I actually aided your cause today—"

"Darla spoke with me as a bud, not as a
counselee! She didn't gloat over your family
problems, either—anything but! She said she
wanted to help you when you were hurting,
Jeff, but you just shut her out. *She came to me
because she was starved for someone to share
her feelings with!*" I paused for a moment and
realized to my horror that Jeff'd just said he
regretted our whole day together. Wounded
deeply, I struck right back. "Of course, after
enduring all those months with *you* as a boyfriend, I'll bet even an ATM would've seemed
like warm company to Darla!"

"Becca!" Kayla gasped, while Jeff's face
turned crimson.

"OH IS THAT SO, YOU DATELESS, PSYCHO-
BABBLING HYPOCRITE?!" he shouted at me.

"Hey, dude, that's south of the border—,"
Zoner protested.

"YES, IT'S SO, YOU SELF-DELUDED, MUD-
SLINGING MEGALOMANIAC!" I screamed right
back as tears began to blur my vision.

"Is there any way to stop 'em once they get going?" Zoner shouted at Kayla.

"NO NEED—I'M OUTTA HERE!" Jeff roared as he wheeled around and charged down the stairs.

Zoner went after Jeff. Kayla went after Zoner. And that left just Roger and me.

My brother went for the door, but I blocked his way and then slammed it shut.

"First you make fun of me for not having a prom date," I seethed as I angrily wiped the wetness from my eyes with the back of my forearm, *"and then you come up here to try to sabotage my last, best chance at one! Well, damn you, we're going to have that little brother-sister chat now, whether you like it or not. Sit down!"*

Roger's eyes flashed with anger and defiance at first, but the more he studied my face, the more the bravado seem to drain out of him, until finally he seemed to despair of escape and instead slumped down on the edge of my bed.

"What have I done to you to make you hate me so much? Why do you want to ruin me?" I asked in a voice hoarse from yelling as I sat down at my desk.

Roger didn't answer for a long time, and when he finally did I had to strain to hear him: "Life totally sucks when everyone thinks your big sister is Ms. Perfecto."

"Everyone? You mean like Jeff Gardiner?"

My brother went on as if he hadn't heard me. " 'Oh, you're so lucky,' people say. 'You can get great advice anytime you want.' But all I get are questions: 'Roger, why are you so moody today? What's with these loser clothes you wear? Can't you find any *decent* friends to hang with? What the hell happened to your hair? Why don't you play the keyboard anymore? Why don't you apply yourself more at school?' *Yak yak yak. Blah blah blah.*"

The world according to Roger Singleton. My first clear look into the murky depths. I took my time absorbing what I was seeing and hearing here, because I really had to get a handle on it this time. I didn't want what'd happened tonight to *ever* happen again.

After many minutes of intense reflection I said, "I can see your point about the clothes, the hair, and to some extent even the friends, Rog. Mom and I are definitely going to have to work harder on giving you your space in those areas. But your moodiness and your laziness are a totally different story. And what *about* school, anyway? Your grades, the vandalism—?"

"You tell me!" he exploded. "You're the expert! God, now that you've been on TV, Luna High'll be *unbearable* for me! 'So, Rog,' they'll ask, 'what's it like to live with a genuine celebrity?' As it is I get crap like: 'Are you *really* Becca's brother, or was there a mix-up at the hospital?'"

I shook my head. "I'm not gonna let you guilt-trip me, bro, so just forget about it. And sure, I'll 'tell you' what I think, only I'm talking as your sister here and not as some sort of 'expert'! I think you basically checked out of life when Dad left, and you've been pissed off at me ever since because *I didn't!* Maybe you've been thinking if you screw up badly enough at Luna High, Mom'll be forced to send you to live with Dad. But that's just not gonna happen. Dad's a great guy, and you know I love him loads, but he simply doesn't have what it takes to go the distance as a full-time parent. He admitted as much at Christmas. *In front of both of us.*"

Roger sat stock-still for a long time.

Eventually his eyes began to well up with tears.

And when I went over to his side and put my arm around him, he didn't pull away.

Instead he told me, in almost a whisper, "After I elbowed you at the mall, I hitched a ride down to the marina with these guys from out of town. We were just screwing around— you know, hopping fences—when two of them jumped me from behind and stole my jacket."

I tensed up, thinking about what *else* could've happened. But Roger didn't need me to spell that out for him. "That must've been awful," I said, holding him a little tighter.

"They knew I wouldn't rat on them to the police, because I was already breaking the law myself. *I am such an idiot! Dad spent a fortune on that jacket, all for me, and now it's gone!*" He started to bawl, and I held him tightly while he cried it out.

"There's no way I can compete with you, Becky," Roger said much later when his eyes were dry again.

"Stop thinking that way," I said. "You're just finishing up the ninth grade. I didn't even get the *idea* for the PCN until the spring of my sophomore year. . . . You'll eventually find your gig, Rog, but you're probably gonna have to bust your butt to make it happen."

He thought about that for a while, and then he sorta grinned at me and said, "My gig, huh? D'you remember when you paid me fifteen bucks to play the keyboard at your thirteenth birthday party? I thought that was a fortune!"

"So did I. But God knows you earned it. What other sixth grader in Luna Point could play the Beach Boys' 'California Girls' and the title song from *Grease* on the same bill?"

We laughed together and started full-on reminiscing about his keyboarding days, until I realized how obscenely late it'd gotten. "I'm majorly sorry for what happened tonight," Roger said contritely as he finally got up to leave. "I hope I haven't totally trashed your prom plans."

"Thanks for the a-a-a-apology, bro." I yawned appreciatively as I retrieved the trash can and carefully peeled Jeff's picture off the bottom. "And don't sweat the prom, 'cause I'm still going, no matter what."

After Roger left I fetched some tape and

made motions to return the photo to the year-book, but then sleep overcame me and I crashed on my bed fully clothed.

I woke up in the morning to find I was clutching Jeff Gardiner's image firmly against my chest.

Chapter 15

I DID SOME CAREFUL bargain-hunting in the week before the prom and finally settled for a pretty white-and-silver dress with a tulle skirt, a genuine steal at just under one hundred dollars. I also bought matching high-heeled shoes and kept the accessorizing simple: a tiny rhinestone choker, bracelets, and earrings. It would've been great to go the more expensive Sylvia Casimiro lace/puffed sleeves/brocade route, but I figured driving into downtown L.A. and forking out 225 bucks for a black leather Hard Rock Cafe jacket was a better investment over the long haul.

Roger sure thought so. When I surprised him with the gift, his eyes opened up like beach umbrellas and he hugged me killer-tight, like he used to when he was a little kid. He even played me a very rusty version of "California Girls" on his newly resuscitated keyboard.

I was now in the process of adjusting my hair color. I knew it was risky, waiting until the morning of prom Saturday to dye my hair, but I figured since I was going to the big dance without a date, it was up to me to generate the magic I'd been counting on. And besides, I desperately wanted to convey to Jeff (who, according to Zoner, was also going to the prom solo) that I was doing just fine without him. Absolutely great, in fact.

I sat on a stool in the bathroom in front of the sink and mirror. I had my hair clipped back on the left side, except for a one-inch-wide strand that I was using to preview the dye. In just a few more minutes, when the egg timer went off, I'd be able to wipe the strand clean and check the results.

Kayla and Zoner'd done their awesome best to bring about a reconciliation between Jeff and me, and it'd almost worked. As a result of gnarly negotiations in which I played only a peripheral role, Jeff met me at the public library after I picked up my paycheck on Friday afternoon. With a preagreement to make no mention (at least at first) of our Wednesday night brawl, we exchanged friendly smiles and walked down to the marina together and out onto the jetty.

The wind was blowing briskly out of the west, and billowing clouds sailed majestically across the azure blue sky, like Yankee clippers bound for Boston. Just off Luna Point a rust red navigation buoy rocked to and fro, clanging out in protest against its heavy burden of dozing harbor seals, which were stacked up like sausages at a Lion's Club charity breakfast.

We watched the waves crash at the jetty's end and marveled at how the spray shimmered in the rays of the setting sun. We could see the surfers taking waves on the beach south of the marina, and Jeff said, only half-teasingly, "I'll bet you'd rather be over there right now."

"You'd lose that bet," I said with a grin as I watched his platinum blond hair whip around in the breeze. He smiled and word-

lessly took my hand in his. Holding his hand
felt amazingly like falling into bed at the end
of a long, exhausting day.

His intense blue eyes gazed into mine, and
he said, "I want to tell you about my parents'
divorce. Would that be okay?"

Would that be okay? Trying hard to contain
my excitement at what this could mean for
him—and for us—I nodded. We found a
huge granite boulder to perch on, and he proceeded to talk. And gesture. And rage! After
a while the pent-up anger, guilt, confusion,
and resentment were just geysering on out,
like spent coolant from an overheated radia-
tor. I'd never felt more close to Jeff than I did
that Friday afternoon.

∾

The egg timer went off.

I wiped the strand clean and examined the
color. Perfect! A pure, true medium brown,
almost exactly as it'd looked on Darla's computer screen. Wasting not a moment, I excitedly mixed the color and developer together
in the applicator bottle, put on the plastic
gloves, placed my right index finger over the
applicator tip, shook the bottle vigorously,

and then began applying it evenly onto my dry hair. When I'd worked it up into a thick, rich lather, I set the egg timer again.

~

When Jeff was done talking, I shared with him how I'd tried to cope with my own parents' divorce. He seemed fascinated by what I had to say and grateful for my reciprocal show of trust. Feeling more confident than ever now about our future prospects, I asked him, "Why blame the therapist for your mom and dad's split when it sounds as if they'd been miserably unhappy with each other for years?"

"Because he made things worse. Along with the blaming business, he put it into my mother's head that she and my father should start *apologizing* to each other. But that was a game my dad wouldn't play."

"It's not a *game,* Jeff," I said, taken aback. "It's as important to be able to say 'I'm sorry' to someone you care about as it is to say 'I love you.'"

"You sound just like my mom! I guess this must be a female thing."

"It is not! C'mon, don't you feel awful about some of the things you said last Wednesday night? I sure do."

"I thought we weren't going to bring that up," he said defensively as he yanked his hand away from mine.

"Not at first, yeah, but *surely* we can talk about it now—"

"There's no point," Jeff said. "Let's leave it in the past where it belongs and move on, okay?"

"But I can't just pretend it didn't happen! I'm *sorry* for the terrible things I said to you, Jeff, and it's important to me that you know that!" I said as I stood up.

"Okay, so I know it now," he said reassuringly as he also stood up. "You want to go to the Jolly Roger for dinner? My treat."

"Don't you have something to say to me first?" I asked with a growing sense of hopelessness.

"Oh, boy," he said, rolling his eyes. "I'm supposed to say 'I'm sorry' now, too, right? But wouldn't my apology seem just a wee bit artificial, seeing as how you had to badger me for it?" Then he smiled as if that'd settled the matter and said, "Hey, I've been thinking a lot about what you said in your presentation, about not having a prom date—"

"You just don't get it, do you?!" I asked in disbelief. "When people apologize, they're showing mutual respect for each other; they're meeting at a halfway point. Don't you respect me?"

"I'm here, aren't I?"

"But that's not enough! I'm here too, *and I also apologized!*"

That was apparently too much for him, and he finally went off on me: "Well then maybe your halfway point is further than I want to go!"

I was devastated.

I turned away from him, choked back a sob, and ran all the way back to my car.

Ding!

I put some warm water in my hair and worked the dye into a lather again. Then I rinsed over and over until the water ran clear. With hardly a pause I picked up the pump spray bottle of highlighter, applied it "generously," per the instructions, to my "clean, damp hair," and then combed it out. After that I picked up my blow-dryer, turned away from the mirror with an ear-to-ear grin (I wanted to surprise myself with the final outcome), and began to blast away. The amazingly swift and simple process of Becca transformation had almost run its course!

What made Jeff's terrible stubbornness all the more ironic in the meantime was the fact that Eddie Ballard had come into my cubicle just two days ago and "surrendered" his tapes of our counseling sessions together. "These belong to you," he said contritely, with almost none of his usual bravado. "I was planning to selectively edit them into a single devastatingly incriminating recording, which I would have then given to Mr. Crampton to use against you, but my heart just wasn't in it. . . . I'm sorry I offended your sensibilities with my prom invitation, by the by."

"Thank you, Eddie," I said uncertainly. I was totally surprised and delighted by his apology and utterly appalled by his plan of revenge.

"Can we still be friends?" he asked in

that anxious, heartbreaking little-boy-lost way of his.

I looked down at the tiny pile of tapes and suddenly saw in it one of those "flashes of promise" I'd told Zoner about. "As a peer counselor I'm big on second chances," I told Eddie with a smile.

"Right-o," he said, smiling back. "By the way, have you been getting enough sleep lately? Your eyes look—"

"I don't want to know," I said firmly.

He nodded and proceeded instead to tell me about a dream involving a fast-moving train, a dark tunnel, and a beautiful conductor named Jennifer, who was actually his lab partner in chemistry. . . .

~

My hair was dry now, so I shut off the blow-dryer and whirled around to get a first look at my new self. But what I saw made me shriek in horror and grab instantly for the bottle of hair lightener. I reread the label at lightning speed. I'd followed the instructions! Every last one of them! But then I read the fine print, which I'd skipped earlier, and found the warning: *"Not recommended for use on color-*

treated hair. Undesirable hues may result." I looked back in the mirror and screamed and then screamed some more at the top of my lungs, until finally my mother and brother burst frantically into the bathroom and demanded to know what was the matter.

I instantly tore a towel off the nearby rack and covered my head with it, but it was too late.

They'd already seen the perfect medium brown hair with the pumpkin orange highlights around the face.

Chapter 16

Mom wouldn't let me recolor it. "You'll have to wait at least a few days, honey; otherwise, you'll irritate your scalp and ruin your hair."

Ruin my hair?!

It was too late to get a wig. And a scarf would only draw more attention to the problem (if such a thing were possible). So that was that.

All was lost.

I couldn't possibly go to the dance now.

Becca Singleton, Prom Night No-Show. Peer Hypocrite.

What would Jeff Gardiner say?!

Still wearing the bath towel ghost-style, I moaned and lay my head down on the counter.

"I think it looks great, Becca," Roger said sincerely. "And original, too—there's only like three other people in the whole school with orange hair."

"That's not the sort of statement your sister was looking to make, honey," Mom told him.

I wondered dully if it was possible to smother yourself with a bath towel, even when your family was watching.

No doubt some medium brown-haired girl with *natural* blond highlights around the face would come up to Jeff at the prom and ask him to dance. They'd hit it off in a major way. No insults, no misunderstandings, no "history." People would watch them with jealous awe and whisper, "Wow, can't you just sense the chemistry? The trust? The mutual respect? And I hear he exchanges apologies with her all the time. . . ."

"I'm calling your friend Kayla right now," Mom said as she gently patted my back. "And

please take that towel off your head before
you smother."

⌐

The last of Kayla's many well-meaning sug-
gestions was to put my hair up in a French
twist and camouflage it with a strategically
assembled crown of California poppies.
"Thanks," I said gratefully, "but I think I'd
prefer to just leave it the way it is, looking like
a shower curtain from the late nineteen
sixties."

"But you can't just give up on the prom
after all you've been through!" Kayla insisted.
"Besides, the dance'll be a total drag without
you there. A *total* drag."

"Kayla, you're really sweet, but get serious.
I look like a walking ad for Minute Maid orange juice. Like I told Zoner not ten minutes
ago: I'll do the hearse, I'll do McDonald's, and
I'll even bowl a few games, if you insist, but
the prom is *absolutely out of the question!*"

A call came in from the Zoneman himself
as we continued to argue while doing our nails
and makeup. Kayla surprised me by insisting
on taking it downstairs, "in private." Since
when did we keep secrets from each other?!

Even worse, when Kayla came back she not only wouldn't talk about the prom anymore but she didn't drop a single hint about what she and Zoner'd discussed. "He just had some last minute questions about wardrobe issues," she said with a smile.

I was already beginning to get that dreaded "third wheel" feeling.

❧

Kayla wore a blue tie-dyed slip dress, black pumps, a black beaded necklace, and sterling silver cresting-wave earrings. Zoner wore black leather flip-flops, white canvas "dress" trunks, a magenta Zog's Sex Wax T-shirt, a tie that was shaped and colored like a surfboard (right down to the sponsor decals) and sported three tiny plastic fins jutting out at the tail, a white Casablanca dinner jacket, a pair of varnished wood-framed sunglasses, and a neon palm tree earring.

Elaine wore a gorgeous blue sequined dress, and Kayla and Zoner promised to stick by her at the dance even if I "flaked out."

The hearse was rather cozier than anyone expected, with its plush purple velvet bench seats and coffin-shaped mahogany table.

Zoner surprised me and Elaine with corsages and then popped the soundtrack from the movie *Grease* into his portable CD player. We all sang along to the title tune (and I thought happily about Roger); Elaine and Kayla howled "Hopelessly Devoted to You" in the manner of two love-struck coyotes; and then Zoner serenaded me with "Beauty School Dropout," with the girls doing background vocals. I was totally mortified at first, but gradually the corny lyrics got to me, and by the end I was singing along, relieved to figure out that this song must've been the innocuous subject of Kayla and Zoner's secretive phone call.

All three of us girls lip-synched "You're the One That I Want" to a cute window attendant at McDonald's, and he rewarded us by doubling up on the fries and tossing in three free hot apple turnovers. "Nice wheels," he said as he handed me the last bag. He must've thought my hair was part of some gimmick, 'cause it didn't seem to faze him in the least.

"To die for," I said in a sultry voice.

The attendant laughed so hard, his headset nearly fell off, and everyone teased me all through dinner about my new Drive-thru Don

Juan, the Fast-Food Figaro, Prince of Packaged Pulp, Connoisseur of Cholesterol.

"Jealousy," I said disdainfully as I waved off their taunts with a Chicken McNugget, "pure jealousy."

Jimmy Buffet, R.E.M., the Trashmen ("Surfin' Bird"), Aerosmith, and the Rivingtons ("Papa-Oom-Mow-Mow") accompanied us on the long haul to the bowling alley in Fountain Valley.

Our formal attire created quite the stir when we arrived and seemed to have a distracting effect on the bowlers in adjacent lanes, especially in one memorable frame when Elaine got her fingers stuck in a ball and it literally tried to score with her.

Overall, though, we girls did pretty well. Poor Zoner, on the other hand, was teased and distracted so relentlessly by his female companions that most of his efforts went into polishing the gutters.

"I hope he dances better than he bowls," Elaine whispered to Kayla and me after the last frame, and then she watched in amazement as we both doubled over with hysterical laughter.

The mood in the hearse had gloomed up

considerably by the time we got back on the San Diego Freeway, southbound. Elaine stared out the window at the passing cars and blurring buildings, her expression now as blue as her dress. Kayla kept giving me sad, sweet, I-can't-believe-this-is-happening-to-my-best-friend looks, while Zoner patted her hand and whispered reassuringly, "Don't stress. It'll be cool, it'll be cool."

"Zoner's right, Kayla—I'll be fine," I finally said out loud. "I had a great time tonight, thanks to you guys. *I really did.*"

She nodded doubtfully.

⌒

Kayla, Zoner, and Elaine made one last desperate plea to me as the hearse pulled up in front of the shimmering lobby doors of the Luna Point Sheraton, promising to guard me from hecklers as conscientiously as Secret Service agents on a presidential detail. By then, though, I was already crouched way down in my seat, begging them to leave as quickly as possible before I was spotted by someone I knew (name: Jeff Gardiner).

Elaine squeezed my hand as she left, and Kayla kissed me on the cheek. Zoner patted me on the shoulder and told me that "orange hair is way more of a turn-on than you realize."

After he shut the door I found myself alone at last, idling in a hearse in front of the junior prom I had so pointlessly fantasized about for months on end. "Take me home, quickly!" I yelped at the driver as the tears began to flow like party punch.

The hearse lurched forward but then screeched to a sudden halt. "What the—!"

Outside, I heard several loud hoots from Zoner, followed by unmistakable shrieks of delight from Kayla and Elaine.

And then the car door opened!

I sat up and shrank back defensively as a big, tuxedo-clad male entered my lair of sorrows.

Jeff Gardiner!

The bane of my existence and the sole object of my thoughts for the past eleven days. Here. In the very same hearse. "I've decided I want to meet you halfway, after all," he said as he sidled up next to me.

Thrilled by his words I turned to take a good, long look at him. I gasped in amazement and then melted like an Eskimo Pie on a summer dashboard. I probably would've fallen hopelessly in love with the guy even if he *hadn't* dyed his hair orange, but that definitely sealed it.

Jeff took me in his arms and kissed me. It was the kind of kiss that was so perfect, so incredibly passionate and heartfelt, it made you want to cry . . . and it tasted like nothing I had ever known before.